The Writers

A Shadow Wars Novella

Kristin Satterfield

WARDEN
BEAR
PRESS

Warden Bear Press

To my muse
(Yes, I mean you James)

Contents

Chapter 1

Amelia

*C**lank stomp clank stomp*

The continuous rhythm of The UnderPod beat in her ears as she lay in her bed. Staring at the ceiling like she did every night, tracing the patterns worn into the dirt, she thought of home. Five years. Five years she had been there, away from all she loved.

One year, *two days and five hours until I'm free,* she thought. The continuous countdown in her head ticked like a clock.

She would be home, at least for a little while, with the sky above her and the earth below where it belonged. She clung to the memories just like she did to the name her parents gave her, Amelia. Just the thought of it—of home—made her long for the days when she would no longer be buried below a mile of dirt and cement, breathing unfiltered air. Even so, she couldn't help but feel trepidation about what it would mean for her.

Unlike many around her, she was not a first-generation Podie. She knew The Pod was training, for what lay ahead. Or rather above. She had seen the changes made to those who emerged from The UnderPod firsthand. On the day he said goodbye to her and her family, before he was sent to the next world, she had seen the way her brother's new legs whirled with gears in his flesh. Ones that gave him speed unlike any other, perfect for a *Runner*. Had seen how her neighbor's little girl wasn't little anymore, her body almost brand new, built for a *Digger*. Leaving The Pod meant changing yourself. *A new step, a new you*, the posters she passed every day said.

She should have been grateful that the change of a *Reader* was small. Just a simple pair of implanted eyes, equipped to ensure one could never miss a detail, would never grow weary in their task. The rumors about the excruciating pain it would bring were rampant, but that was the least of her worries. No, what kept her up on nights like tonight, tossing and turning, were the rumors that floated along the deepest parts of The Pod. The ones that no one would speak out loud in the light, only through whispers in dark times when people slept. About the ones who failed the test.

No one knew what the tests were, just that they were required by every Podie before they could leave for The Next World. She had heard once from her bunk neighbor #409 that #409 had heard they tested for *writers*. The word was spoken so quickly, so low, that Amelia was almost unsure whether she had heard 409 correctly.

Writers, the very word was forbidden. Few people even knew what it meant, fewer still what they could do. But she knew. Her grandfather, a man she never met, had been a writer, and her father as well, before they had taken him away and equipped him for reading. She could remember stories that her father used to tell her at night. Not all of them, but there were bits and pieces. Things about knights and wars, and revolution.

He told her about writers. How they weaved stories, ones about things new and old, things real and unreal. They were so powerful that even a few simple lines could topple entire governments if they wanted to. It's why they were deemed too dangerous for the Next World. Their existence was erased from the histories.

Yet, secretly she had always wanted to be a writer.

A shrill noise broke through the rhythm in the background of her mind and woke her from her thoughts. It was time to work. She dragged herself out of the bed and plopped down onto the floor.

3

"Watch it," her bunkmate #556 said as she barely missed her head. "You're not some freaking Killer you know." *Killers* now that was a job coveted above all else. Rarer and more revered than *Readers*. They trained day and night, harder than the *Runners*, *Throwers*, and *Players*. Few people knew what they truly did, but one thing was certain. *Killers* were scary. As graceful as cats and as quiet as mice, they could take out a person in under a second. Next to being a *Writer*, she saw it as one of the best jobs. She wasn't alone. Many people longed to be *Killers*, and they treated those who were with great respect.

She dragged herself along the room full of bunk beds, grabbing her grey sweatpants and baggy, worn t-shirt from her cubby at the end. The clothes of a reader. Others stirred around her, hands grabbing their own uniforms above and beside as they scrambled to be on time. Following the crowd out of the brown building she was in, she headed towards the showers. It was always the same day and night; nothing ever changed. Wash, dress, eat, work, eat, sleep, repeat. The flow of people through The UnderPod like blood pumping through a brown dirt-covered heart.

Above her was darkness, the ceiling of The UnderPod somewhere stories above the tallest of the buildings, the settlement buried deep in the earth. Perfectly packed dirt lay below her, and her movement didn't kick up a single speck. Around her were grey, brown, and silver bland buildings.

That day as the group passed by Sector 99, she lingered behind. Maybe it was because she dreamed of the surface again, maybe it was because something in her bones itched that day—she didn't know. Sector 99 was where the *Killers* trained. She watched them from afar, admiring their grace and strength, with a longing in her heart. *Killers* had a different attitude than anyone in The Pod. There was something about the way they walked and talked that suggested that they knew more and had seen more than anyone else, even the *Readers*. She wished she could be like that.

As Amelia turned to join her group before they got too far, a crash emanated from behind her. She spun in time to see a door across the yard fall off its hinges, dust and debris flying as it landed. From admits the cloud rushed a boy. By the looks of him, he was no older than she was. His body was well built, like any other *Killer*, and his hair was a light blond, lighter than any she had ever seen. She didn't know what it was about him, but there was something different. His very presence seemed to bring light to dark and dusty Pod. So much so that she realized she had never noticed how dark it had been until she saw him.

The boy looked around the clearing, his eyes blazing, seeming to stop when he spotted her. A commotion was audible to him from within the building behind him. The group training on the ground in front of him turned to watch, confused. The crowd around Amelia had stopped, their daily routine interrupted by the strange events. In one swift movement that almost seemed like a blur, the boy was running towards the crowd, towards her. The surrounding people screeched and darted away, but she didn't move. Pinned down by the determined look in his eyes. In seconds he was on her. She felt something brush against her hand and caught three words whispered in her ear, sending shivers down her spine before he was forcefully dragged away by The Patrol.

"Keep this safe."

Amelia stood in a daze watching as the boy was taken away, his arms twisted painfully behind his back. It wasn't until they had dragged him back into the building and The Patrol had ushered the crowd on their way that she registered the feeling of the paper in her hand. She had always been a rule follower. She had never disobeyed except in her desire to be a writer. Yet, when The Patrol passed by, she shoved the paper into her pants and continued following the crowd, pretending for all the world like everything was normal. She couldn't take a shower; she knew that. Once she stripped, someone would find the paper and punish her. She had only minutes to come up with an excuse. By the time she arrived at the washhouse, she had her escape planned.

"Move along," ordered the gruff voice of a *Patrol* as he stood above them, taking the normal spot of the soft-spoken women that usually guarded the washhouse. Relief flooded her when she saw him. Her old plan was gone, and a new one formed. She stopped at the door and veered right instead of left. Right before she passed through the doors, a calloused hand caught her arm.

"Where do you think you are going?" The *Patrol* demanded, glaring down at her.

"Sir?" she asked him, playing coy.

"The washhouse and showers are through that door," the man said.

Amelia faked an embarrassed expression, looking down at her feet. "I know, sir, but I am not allowed in the wash-house at this time."

"What do you mean?" he demanded.

Keeping up her act, she pointed to the sign above the door.

The man looked up, and seeing the sign for the first time, his face turned scarlet. "Oh, carry on," he said, letting her go. She smiled to herself as she passed through the door. This section of the washhouse was for those who were experiencing their monthly cycle. The man was so flustered that she knew he wouldn't check to see if she was even supposed to be there.

Luckily, she was alone when she arrived. She stripped quickly, hiding the paper in her clean clothes.

When she was done and dressed in clean clothes, with the paper transferred to the space between her breasts, Amelia joined the crowd exiting the washhouse heading to work. The crowd thinned as she headed to Sector 100, and soon it was just her and the ten other *Readers*. She knew some of them well and would, even under torture, call them friends. One such friend, # 770, waved to her, and she nodded to him with a small smile. Once inside the building, she split off from the group, heading to her per-spective room. The best thing about being a *Reader* was the privacy. The officers left them alone in their rooms to read. Their freedom came with trust, trust that the *Read-ers* would finish their work and not complain. Trust that no funny business or problems would arise from them. Trust that they would always stay in line. Not that they would ever slack off. Every *Reader* liked his / her job and wanted to keep it.

Many people often wondered what the *Readers* read if no one wrote for them. The answer was a lot. Where it came from, no one bothered to ask. Official documents, historical papers, declarations and decrees—all these things the *Readers* read and all these things they understood. Some Readers held the high honor of also becoming *Speakers*. The ones who bring the words to the population during town halls and city parades. Others, however, were *Dictators*, helping the *Speakers* know what to say and when to say it.

Shutting the door behind her, Amelia quickly rushed to her table. She was the fastest Reader in history and always had free time when she was done with her work. It was one reason she had the biggest room and a personal library to fill the void. So when she went through her work in record time, she didn't even notice. The piece of paper in her shirt was burning a hole in her chest. As she read the last line of the day, she quickly pulled it out as she shoved her work aside. Inspecting the paper, she noticed it was not one, but many pieces folded and stuck together. Slowly she unfolded them, careful not to rip them, treating them like treasured gold. She then separated the pieces and laid them out on the table around her.

Someone scrawled the words on the paper in an uneven form, with some letters bigger than others, and some more slanted or smudged. They were unlike other words she had read. Those words were clean, crisp, and straight.

The rough font in front of her was more interesting and exciting than her usual work. In a way, they reminded her of her own secret works, though messier, as if done by an unpracticed and unsteady hand.

Slowly and carefully, she read.

She soon became engrossed in the work. There were words in the story that she did not know. Words like war, hate, death, and sadness. She had heard of some of them before. They had been part of old stories her father told in the night. Words that he had thrown about before the *Reconstruction*. But she had never known their meaning, too young. Finally, her eyes fell on the last page, and her face creased even more in confusion. Her heart stopped as she finally read the last sentence.

A knock at the door made her jump.

"Hey there. It's me, #809. I was wondering if you want to go to dinner with me during free time," called a male voice from the other side of the door. She took a breath, her heart still beating fast. #809 was a good friend who shared the room nearby. He was handsome, or at least that's what everyone said, and he had often come to her for advice and a friendly conversation. #300 had once told her that #809 liked her. She hadn't believed her until #809 had started going out of his way to find her. He was a nice guy, but she was unsure of her feelings for him. It was out of respect that she answered his advances with a yes.

Amelia was about to tell him to wait at the doors like he always did when she stopped. The bright blond-headed boy from this morning popped into her mind, and she couldn't bring herself to speak the words.

"You know, 809, I'm not feeling well today. I think I will turn in early. Thank you for asking," she replied, trying to keep her voice even.

"Oh, that's alright," he said, and she caught the disappointment in his tone. "I'll see you tomorrow, 666." And with that, he left.

666.

The number made her heart skip a beat as she looked back at her desk and the paper that lay there. The last section seemed to pop off the page, taunting her. She stared at it again, her mind trying to understand what it meant. Finally, with a sigh, she grabbed the papers and shoved them in her desk drawer, where she hid all the stories she had illegally written, and locked it behind her. As she left Building 100 and headed home, the words continued to ring in her ears.

666, with the numbers of the devil the righteous shall be set free and the blind will see. By her word, *she will lead them. The revolution shall begin.*

Chapter 2

Elias

E lias Marlowe sat at his desk, the soft glow of his lamp casting a warm light over the pages scattered before him. His brow furrowed over deep-set brown eyes as he reread the latest draft of his essay, his olive-toned fingers absently tracing the intricate patterns on the worn leather cover of his journal.

He had been working tirelessly for weeks, meticulously crafting his words to convey the depth of his research and the nuances of his arguments. As a *Writer*, Elias took pride in his ability to weave together complex ideas and present them in a way that was both intellectually engaging and emotionally resonant.

But tonight, something was off. A nagging feeling of unease had been gnawing at the back of his mind, a persistent distraction that he couldn't quite shake. He set down his pen and leaned back in his chair, running a hand through his tousled hair.

Elias knew that the society of Univocan was not without its flaws. As an observer and chronicler of its history, he had witnessed the cracks in the veneer of perfection that the government so carefully maintained. The rigid adherence to order, the suppression of individuality, the control over information— these were the things that troubled him, even as he outwardly conformed to the expectations of his role.

But tonight, the unease was different, more acute. It was as if a subtle shift had occurred, a tremor in the foundations of the world he knew. Elias couldn't quite put his finger on it, but the feeling persisted, a whisper that demanded his attention.

He glanced down at the pages before him; the words blurring together as his mind raced. What was it that was troubling him so? Was it something he had missed in his research, some crucial detail that had eluded him?

Elias sighed, running a hand down his trimmed beard, and pushed his chair back, rising to his feet. He needed to clear his head, to step away from the confines of his study and reconnect with the world beyond his books. Perhaps a walk through the streets of Univocan, a chance to observe the rhythm of the city, would provide the clarity he sought.

As he stepped out into the cool night air, Elias couldn't help but feel a sense of unease. Around him, the towering buildings of glass and metal glowed red and yellow from windows of others awake, yet the streets were eerily quiet, the usual hum of activity muted and subdued. He quickened his pace, his eyes scanning the shadows for any sign of movement. The tight spaces between the buildings of his sector made travel by anything other than foot impossible; even then, some alleyways weren't meant to be traversed.

And then, in the distance, he heard it—a faint whisper, a barely audible murmur that sent a chill down his spine. Elias paused, straining to hear, his heart pounding in his chest.

The words were indistinct, but the tone was unmistakable—a note of urgency, a plea for help.

Elias felt a surge of adrenaline as he turned and hurried towards the source of the sound, his mind racing with a thousand questions. *What was happening? Who was in trouble? And what could he do to help?*

He quickened his pace, his heart pounding. As he turned the corner, he glimpsed a figure in the distance, hunched over and seemingly in distress. He hesitated for a moment, his natural caution warring with his desire to help. But the sight of the person's obvious struggle spurred him forward, and he hurried to close the distance.

"Excuse me, are you alright?" Elias called out, his voice cutting through the stillness of the night.

The figure startled and turned to face him, and Elias felt a surge of recognition. It was Rafe, a young *Reader* whom Elias had worked with in the past, his dark features etched with fear and desperation, light brown eyes shining with unshed tears.

"You must help me," Rafe pleaded, his voice barely above a whisper. "They're coming, and I don't know what to do."

Elias reached out a steadying hand, his brow furrowed with concern. "Who's coming? What's happening?"

Rafe glanced nervously over his shoulder, his eyes darting back and forth. "The Patrol," he hissed. "They're after me, and I can't—" His words were cut off by the sudden sound of footsteps, and Elias felt a chill run down his spine. He turned to see a group of uniformed figures approaching, their faces obscured by the shadows.

One of the Patrol members shouted, "There he is!" Elias realized they had been spotted.

Without hesitation, he grabbed the young man's arm and pulled him into a nearby alleyway, shielding him from view. His heart raced as he listened to the Patrol members draw closer, their voices echoing through the narrow passage.

"Where did he go?" one of them demanded.

Elias held his breath, praying that the darkness would conceal them. Rafe trembled beside him, his eyes wide with fear.

Then, just as The Patrol members were about to turn the corner, a loud commotion erupted from the opposite end of the alley. Elias and the young man both startled, their heads snapping towards the source of the noise. The Patrol turned toward their alley to inspect it, and Elias knew he needed to act. Without a moment's hesitation, he stepped out of their hiding spot into the alley, his hands raised in a gesture of surrender.

"Excuse me, officers," he called out, his voice projecting an air of calm authority. "Is there a problem?"

The Patrol members whirled around, their eyes narrowing as they took in Elias' appearance. "You there, citizen," one of them barked. "Have you seen a young man pass through here? He's wanted for questioning."

Elias schooled his features, projecting an air of innocence. "I'm afraid I haven't seen anyone," he replied evenly. "I was simply out for an evening stroll when I heard the commotion. Is everything alright?"

The Patrol members exchanged skeptical glances, but Elias could see the uncertainty in their eyes. They were clearly caught off guard by his calm demeanor and cooperative attitude.

"Keep your eyes open," the lead Patrol member growled, gesturing to his companions. "He couldn't have gone far."

As The Patrol members turned and hurried down the alley, Elias let out a silent sigh of relief. He quickly ducked back into the shadows, rejoining Rafe who was trembling with fear.

"It's alright," Elias whispered, placing a reassuring hand on the man's shoulder. "They're gone for now, but we need to move quickly."

Rafe nodded, his eyes darting nervously around the alley. "Thank you," he breathed, his voice barely audible. "I don't know what I would have done if you hadn't..."

Elias raised a hand, silencing the man. "We can discuss that later," he murmured. "Right now, we need to find a safe place to hide."

Without another word, Elias led the young man deeper into the alley, his mind racing. He couldn't shake the feeling that this chance encounter was more than just a random incident—there was something larger at play, something that was unraveling the carefully constructed fabric of Univocan society.

As they rounded a corner, Elias spotted a small, nondescript door set into the side of a building he recognized. He paused, considering their options. Was it worth the risk to reveal one of his hidden alcoves? The answer was yes. It always was when it came to the safety of others, something that drove his family insane.

"This way," he whispered, guiding Rafe towards the door. "We should be able to hide here for a moment." Elias pressed his hand against the door, and to his relief, it swung open silently. He ushered the young man inside, then quickly closed the door behind them, sealing them off from the outside world.

The air of the abandoned lower-level apartment was stale. The room was dimly lit, but Elias could make out the outlines of his simple furnishings—a table, a couple of chairs, and a small cot in the corner. He gestured for Rafe to take a seat, then paced the small space, his mind racing.

"What is going on, Rafe?" he asked, his voice low and urgent. "And why is The Patrol after you?"

The young man shifted nervously in his chair, his eyes darting around the room. "I... I'm not sure why they're after me. I was just trying to deliver a message, and I..." His voice trailed off, and he shook his head, his face etched with fear.

Elias frowned, his brow furrowing with concern. "A message? What kind of message?"

Rafe hesitated, then reached into his pocket and pulled out a folded piece of paper. "This," he said, his voice barely audible. "I was supposed to deliver it to someone, but now..." He shook his head again, his eyes pleading.

Elias took the paper, his fingers trembling slightly as he unfolded it. His eyes scanned the unfamiliar words, his heart pounding in his chest. "What is this?" he breathed, his gaze locked on the page. He felt a surge of adrenaline coursing through his veins.

Rafe leaned forward, his eyes wide. "I don't know," he whispered. "But it's important; I know it is. And now The Patrol is after me, and I don't know what to do."

Elias looked up, his eyes meeting Rafe's. "We need to get you somewhere safe. More permanent than this," he said, his voice firm. "And then we can figure out what this means."

Rafe nodded, his expression one of relief and gratitude. "Thank you," he whispered. "I... I don't know what I would have done without you."

Elias placed a hand on Rafe's shoulder, his gaze steady and reassuring. "We'll figure this out," he said, determined. "But we need to hurry. The Patrol won't stop searching for you. Do you have any place you can hide, somewhere they won't think to look?"

Rafe shook his head, his eyes downcast. "I... I don't. Not since Jenn..." His voice cracked before he took a deep breath. "Maybe the person I was going to meet could help. But I'm not sure how to find them now."

Elias frowned in thought. Glancing around the small room, his eyes landed on a narrow staircase tucked into the corner.

"There might be a way to get you out of the city without The Patrol finding you. From there, maybe you can find this contact again."

Rafe hesitated for a moment, then nodded and rose to his feet, his movements cautious. Elias led the way, his footsteps light as they ascended the stairs. The passage was cramped, but he pressed on, his senses heightened as he scanned the area for any signs of danger.

As they reached the top of the stairs, Elias paused, his hand on the doorknob. "Stay close to me," he whispered, "and be ready to move quickly."

Rafe nodded, his expression tense. Taking a deep breath, Elias slowly pushed open the door, peering out into the dimly lit alleyway beyond. Satisfied that the coast was clear, he gestured for Rafe to follow him, and the two men slipped out into the late night. He knew the upper streets well, having explored them countless times during his evening walks. But tonight, the familiar paths felt foreign and treacherous, the shadows seeming to harbor unseen dangers. As they turned a corner, Elias glimpsed movement in the distance. He quickly ushered Rafe into a nearby doorway, shielding him from view.

"Stay here," he whispered, his voice low and urgent. "I'll go check it out."

Rafe nodded, his eyes wide with fear, and Elias stepped out from the doorway, his senses on high alert. From down the alleyway, a hooded figure emerged. Elias froze in place, like a deer in headlights.

"The sword is a powerful weapon, striking down all those in its path," the hooded figure's voice called out in the night, soft-spoken yet hitting Elias like a train.

"What—"

"Yet, the pen is mightier than the sword." Rafe said from behind Elias, cutting him off and sending him spinning. The young man stood before him, his expression a mix of fear and determination.

"What do you mean?" Elias asked, his voice barely above a whisper.

Rafe glanced nervously towards the hooded figure, then back at Elias. "It's a code... the message," he said, his voice trembling slightly. "This is the man I was supposed to meet. Or at least someone who knows the code."

Elias felt a chill run down his spine. "But how?"

Rafe opened his mouth to respond, but before he could, the hooded figure stepped forward, his features still obscured by the shadows.

"The revolution is coming," the figure said, his voice low and measured. "And you, Elias Marlowe, have a choice to make a difference."

Elias felt his heart skip a beat. How did this stranger know his name? And what did he mean by a revolution?

"I don't understand," he said, his brow furrowed in confusion. "What revolution? And what does it have to do with me?"

The hooded figure stepped closer, and Elias glimpsed his face—it was a man, his features weathered and his eyes burning with an intensity that sent a shiver down his spine.

"A revolution that will challenge the very foundations of Univocan society," the man said, his voice unwavering. "You are someone who understands Univocan better than most. Know what it lacks and what it has in abundance. Where to chop it down and where to help it grow."

Elias opened his mouth to respond, but the man raised a hand, silencing him.

"The message you now hold," he continued, "is the key to unlocking the truth. But be warned—the path ahead is fraught with danger. The Patrol will stop at nothing to silence those who dare to challenge the status quo."

The implications of the man's words were staggering, and Elias couldn't help but feel a sense of both fear and excitement. It was like someone had dug deep into his mind, to the thoughts he refused to entertain about the city, about their society, and placed them before him.

"What am I supposed to do?" he asked, his voice barely above a whisper.

The hooded figure stepped back, his expression obscured once more by the shadows. "That, my friend, is for you to decide. If you wish to know more, leave your favorite pen on your windowsill; our people will find you," he said. With those words, the man turned and disappeared into the darkness, leaving Elias and Rafe alone in the alley, their minds reeling with the weight of what had just been revealed.

Elias turned to Rafe, his eyes searching the young man's face. "What have we gotten ourselves into?" he asked, his voice laced with uncertainty.

Rafe shook his head, his expression a mix of fear and resolve. "I don't know," he said, his voice barely audible. "But I know you've felt it too. The way the society is breaking at the seams. The way the shadows seem to linger, to grow now. Elias, we can't let it go unanswered. Whatever is wrong, whatever the source of this feeling is, we should root it out before it can rot all we have built."

Elias hesitated, his mind racing. The prudent course of action would be to distance himself from this entire situation, to return to the safety and comfort of his familiar life. But deep within him, something refused to let go—a curiosity and a sense of duty that compelled him to uncover the truth.

"Alright," Elias said, his voice steady despite the turmoil raging within. "Let's get you to safety first."

The two men set off, their footsteps quick and purposeful. The alleyways grew narrower and more winding, and Elias couldn't shake the feeling that they were being watched. After what felt like a lifetime, they made to the second of three of Elias's hidden dens. Quickly making sure no one was watching, he ushered Rafe into the space.

"No one knows about this place. You should be safe here for a few days," he explained as he turned the lights on, revealing a small living space equipped with an icebox, food, and a small bathroom to the side. "I'm scheduled to fly out to Luna Prime next week for a semipermanent assignment. I'll see if I can manage to get you registered on board. I know a Writer who's good at that sort of thing, and they owe me a favor." With a sigh, Elias ran his hand through his hair, tousling it more than it already was. "Guess this works out for both of us. I wasn't going to have time to empty this place out and the preservation bots will be expiring in a month or so. Feel free to make yourself at home." Not knowing what else to say or do, he turned back to the door.

"Elias."

Rafe's voice stopped his hand on the doorknob, the door open only a crack.

"Yes?" he asked, glancing over his shoulder to the young man.

Rafe shuffled nervously before looking up. "Thank you." His sincerity, tone and eyes rang with a sincerity that thawed the regret growing in Elias's heart.

"You're welcome."

Chapter 3

Darius

D arius strode through the bustling streets of New Horizon, his black uniform crisp and his blue-eyed gaze sharp and alert. As a *Killer*, he was responsible for maintaining order and enforcing Univocan laws within the Martian colony. It was a role he took immense pride in, for he believed deeply in the principles that guided their society. Darius had grown up on Mars, his parents having been among the first wave of colonists to settle the harsh, alien world. From a young age, he had trained to be strong, disciplined, and uncompromising in his dedication to the greater good. The *Killer* program had honed his skills, turning him into a formidable warrior capable of handling any threat that arose. As he made his rounds that day, Darius nodded to the citizens he passed, acknowledging their greetings with a brief nod. The people of New Horizon respected the *Killers*, knowing that their presence ensured the safety and stability of the colony. It was a trust he was careful not to abuse.

His attention was drawn to a commotion up ahead. Quickening his pace, Darius approached the scene, his bronze hand resting lightly on the hilt of his sidearm. A small crowd gathered around two individuals, their voices raised in heated discussion. Darius stepped forward, his imposing presence immediately commanding the attention of the onlookers, who parted for him like the Red Sea. "What's going on here?" he asked, his voice calm but firm.

One individual, a young man with a defiant expression, turned to face Darius. "Nothing that concerns you, Killer," he spat.

Darius raised an eyebrow, surprised but undeterred by the man's hostility. "I'm afraid it does concern me if there is a disturbance in the colony. Now, I suggest you both calm down and explain what the issue is."

The other individual, a woman with a worried expression, stepped forward. "I'm sorry, Killer Kane. This is just a... misunderstanding between myself and my colleague. We'll resolve it privately."

Darius studied the two for a moment, his keen eyes assessing the situation. He could sense an undercurrent of tension, but the woman's conciliatory tone suggested that the matter was not serious enough to warrant his intervention. Nodding, he stepped back, his hand leaving the hilt of his sidearm.

"Very well. See that it is resolved quickly and without further incident. I don't want to have to come back here." With that, Darius continued on his patrol, his mind already refocusing on the tasks at hand. He was confident that the people of New Horizon understood the importance of maintaining order and that they would heed his warning.

As the day wore on, Darius carried out his duties with his usual efficiency and professionalism. He responded to minor disturbances, assisted citizens with various requests, and oversaw the security checks at the colony's main entrance. It was a routine that he had grown accustomed to, one that he took pride in even if it got repetitive. However, as the afternoon drew to a close, Darius found himself drawn to a particular area of the colony that he had not visited in some time. The Habitat District, where the *Writers* lived and worked, was a quiet space. Water fountains lined the paths, soft grass and patches of places to sit and think under majestic oak trees scattered the space. His shoulder relaxed subconsciously the moment he stepped in.

Darius noticed another crowd gathered outside one of the larger residential buildings. Curious, as it was the second time such a thing had happened that day, one incident an unusual occurrence in itself, he quickened his pace, his instincts on high alert. When he reached the crowd, he was surprised to see a group of *Killers*, their weapons drawn, surrounding a lone individual who was being escorted away. He had never received a call for an arrest over his com. He pushed his way through the onlookers, his brow furrowed in confusion.

"What's going on here?" he demanded, his voice commanding attention.

One of the *Killers*, a veteran named Jansen, turned to face him. "Killer Kane," he said, his tone grave. "We've apprehended a Writer who was caught attempting to destroy government property."

Darius's eyes widened, his gaze shifting to the individual being led away. He was a man with dark skin and light brown eyes. He recognized him, though he couldn't recall his name. "A Writer?" he said, his voice tinged with disbelief. "Surely there must be some mistake."

Jansen shook his head. "I'm afraid not, Killer Kane. We caught him red-handed trying to sabotage the colony's data archives. This is a serious offense against Univocan."

Darius felt a knot forming in the pit of his stomach. The idea of a *Writer*, someone entrusted with the preservation of their society's history and culture, committing such a crime was unfathomable to him.

"Have you informed the government?" Darius asked, his voice low. His shoulders tensed with the ramifications of what this could mean for the peace of the colony.

"Yes, the appropriate authorities have been notified," Jansen replied. "They'll be handling the investigation and the sentencing."

Darius nodded, his mind racing. He knew that the punishment for such an offense would be severe. As he watched the man being led away, a sense of unease took hold. "Understood. Let me know how I can be of assistance."

"You're a good man, Kane." Jansen clasped Darius's shoulder with a firm, pale hand, before he turned and followed the other Killers away. "For now keep to your normal duties; let us in the higher ranks worry about this."

Darius nodded and tried to go back to his normal routine, but something was bugging him. A part of him couldn't help but wonder if there was more to the story. *Writers* were not known for acts of defiance or subversion—they were the keepers of Univocan's legacy, dedicated to their work with a reverence that bordered on veneration. They were passive individuals, usually lost in their minds and their dreams more than the surrounding realities.

Darius found himself drawn to the Habitat District once more. His fingers flying across his PortMed on his wrist, the holographic band opened with information only he could see. The name of the *Writer* was Jonal, and it was then Darius remembered who he was. He had met Jonal and his mentor, Elias, a few months back when they had arrived with the latest caravan from Luna Prime. Elias was a solar renowned *Writer*, entrusted above all others with the most important information of Univocan. Darius had quickly found him to be an enjoyable, inelegant man who was willing to part with thoughts of wisdom. Though he was supposed to be impartial to all citizens, he found he had a soft spot for the middle-aged man.

Why would a *student of such a man try to destroy everything his mentor stood for?* He needed to understand what had driven this *Writer* to such a drastic act.

Stepping into the residential building where Jonal resided, Darius made his way to the *Writer's* apartment, his mind working overtime. When he reached the door, he paused, his hand hovering over the access panel. He knew he should report his concerns to the authorities and let them handle the investigation; it was what he would have done in any other circumstance, but a part of him screamed to stay quiet.

With a deep breath, Darius activated the panel and stepped inside, his eyes scanning the modest but well-appointed living space. It was a far cry from the spartan accommodations he was accustomed to, and he couldn't help but feel a sense of curiosity about the individual who had called this place home. As he moved deeper into the apartment, Darius's gaze was drawn to a desk in the corner, where a stack of papers and a well-worn journal lay. Intrigued, he approached the desk, his fingers tracing the weathered cover of the journal.

He hesitated for a moment, his sense of duty warring with his growing curiosity. He knew he shouldn't be tampering with evidence, but the allure of uncovering the truth was too strong to resist. With a resigned sigh, he opened the journal and read.

The words on the page were eloquent and thoughtful, reflecting a depth of insight that Darius had not expected. The Writer had written extensively about his observations of Univocan society, his concerns about the government's increasingly restrictive policies, and his belief that the people were being denied the freedom to truly live.

Darius felt a strange sense of unease as he continued to read, his understanding of the world he had always known beginning to shift. The words painted a picture of a society that was not as perfect as Darius had always believed, one where individual expression and dissent were suppressed in the name of order and efficiency. The more he read, the more he questioned. He had always believed that the *Killers* were the guardians of Univocan, tasked with maintaining the stability and prosperity that had made their society the envy of the known world. But now, he found himself confronted with facts in black and white stating multiple instances where they were used as points of violence, of oppression. He was suddenly faced with the possibility that the government he had sworn to serve was not as benevolent as he had been led to believe.

Or it could all be lies. He thought. Darius's hand trembled slightly as he turned the pages, his mind racing with the implications of what he had discovered. The words on the very last page of the journal froze his shaking hands.

No. The word resounded in his mind as he read the two words again.

Elias Marlowe.

The journal didn't belong to Jonal.

Suddenly, a noise from outside the apartment startled Darius, causing him to snap the journal shut and quickly shove it into his storage belt. The item sucked into the void, the space created, a tiny space warp for storage, appearing with a small ping in the corner of his eyesight among the list of other items it stored. He listened intently, his senses heightened, and his hand instinctively reached for his sidearm.

After a few tense moments, Darius realized that it had been nothing more than the sound of the building's ventilation system kicking in. Letting out a slow breath, he turned his attention back to the empty room, the realization of what he had just done dawning on him. Reaching to his PortMed to call the journal back into his hands and return it to its place on the table, he paused. He couldn't simply ignore what he had discovered. The implications were too profound, and the potential consequences too severe. He had to decide—would he report his findings to the authorities, as was his duty, or would he find a way to protect Jonal, Elias and the truths he had uncovered?

And would doing so compromise all that I am? He couldn't help but wonder. The weight of his decision pressed down on him like lead.

The sound of footsteps approaching the apartment decided it for him. Quickly, he moved away from the desk, his heart racing as he prepared to confront whoever entered. To Darius's relief, it was not a member of the government's security forces, but rather a young woman—a *Writer*, judging by her attire. She paused when she saw him, her eyes widening with a mixture of surprise and apprehension.

"Killer Kane," she said, her voice trembling slightly. "What are you doing here?"

Darius hesitated for a moment, unsure of how to respond. He knew he had to tread carefully, as any misstep could potentially put Elias's life in danger.

"I was... investigating a disturbance in the area," he replied, his tone measured and calm. "I'm afraid I can't discuss the details with you, but I assure you that everything is under control."

The woman eyed him warily, her gaze flickering briefly to the desk where the journal once lay. "I see," she said, her voice barely above a whisper. "Well, I'll be on my way, then."

Darius nodded, watching as the woman hurried past him and out of the apartment. He knew that he would have to be vigilant, as word of his presence here would likely spread quickly among the *Writers*. Careful to act as normal as he could, he left the room, walking down the long hall and out of the residence. He had almost made it to the central plaza when the call of his name stopped him.

"Killer Kane," Jansen said, his brow furrowed with concern. "We've been looking for you. There's been a... development in the investigation."

Darius felt a knot forming in the pit of his stomach as he turned, his gaze meeting Jansen's. "What kind of development?" he asked, his voice betraying a hint of trepidation.

Jansen hesitated for a moment, his expression grave. "It appears that the Writer we apprehended earlier has... disappeared."

Darius's eyes widened, his mind racing with the implications of Jansen's words. "Disappeared?" he echoed, his voice tinged with disbelief as he fought not to portray the relief he felt. "How is that possible?"

Jansen shook his head, his frustration evident. "We're not sure, but the authorities are launching a full-scale investigation. They've asked that all Killers in the area assist in the search."

Darius nodded, his mind already planning how to use this development to his advantage. "Of course," he said, his voice steady. "I'll join the search immediately."

As he followed Jansen out of the Habitat District, Darius's thoughts were still ragged, tangled by the revelations he had just learned. Though his world was slowly falling apart around him, he knew he had to find Elias. He would make him answer all the questions in his head, and if the man spoke the truth, he would help him fix their world before it could fall apart. After all, he was a *Killer*, his only role in life was to ensure the prosperity of the Univocan people at any cost.

Chapter 4

Ava

Ava's tan fingers gripped the worn leather of her journal, the pages filled with a series of letters she had been carefully composing under old man Elias' guidance. She sat cross-legged on the dirt floor of their modest hideout, the flickering light of a single lantern casting shadows across her face. Her connection to The Underground and unwavering spirit made her the ideal messenger, and the rebellion had chosen her for this mission. Yet the weight of it was a burden she wasn't sure she could bear. There was so much that depended on her and her writings, so much that could go wrong or right. Taking a deep breath, Ava wrote, her pen gliding across the paper with purpose.

Dear 666,

I hope this letter reaches you safely, hidden within the shadows of The UnderPod. My name is Ava, and I am part of the resistance, The Unbound—those who refuse to accept the government's grip on our lives.

I know what it feels like to live in fear, trapped inside a system designed to control every thought, every movement. But I want you to know that you are not alone. There are many of us out here fighting for your freedom—and for the return of something precious that was stolen from us: the power of the written word.

We have not forgotten the Writers, nor the knowledge and stories they once shared. Their words inspired generations, and their absence has left a silence that echoes through every corner of Univocan.

Elias, a dear friend and one of our leaders, has entrusted me with these letters. Each one carries a piece of the truth—and a piece of the plan we hope will awaken something within you and others like you. He believes that your voice, your creativity, and your courage could be the spark that reignites what has been lost. That spark is rare now, especially among the younger generations, and it is why you matter so deeply to this cause.

In this first letter, I want to give you a glimpse of life beyond the UnderPod and the Next World. Out here, we live freely—by our own rules, following our own paths. We've learned to find joy in the simple things the government has stripped away. We don't have the comforts of the cities, but what we do have is far more valuable: choice.

It may be hard to imagine, but there is a world where you are not defined by your assigned role—a world where you can explore your passions and truly discover who you are. Out here, we write our own stories, not the ones dictated to us by the system.

Hold on to that dream, 666. Keep it alive within you, even when the darkness closes in. As long as there are people willing to fight for freedom, that dream will never die.

I will continue to send letters, each carrying messages of hope and fragments of our plan. Trust that we are working tirelessly to find a way to breach the walls of The UnderPod and bring our people back to the surface—to a life where words and choice belong to everyone again.

Until then, stay strong, keep your heart open, and remember: the future is closer than you think.

Yours in the struggle for freedom,
Ava

Ava paused, reading over the words. She knew that the first letter was crucial, setting the tone and laying the groundwork for the messages to come. Frustrated, she made to crumble the letter but paused. It was not a bad letter, but she knew it was not quite enough. Something important, something key, was missing, and since she was not a *Writer* like Elias or a *Speaker* like her husband, she wasn't sure she could figure out what it was.

"What would entice a Reader who has known and read all knowledge available to her? That has never needed for anything. What would make her pause, not report, but consider?" she wondered out load, speaking into the vast empty wasteland that lay past the window before her.

"For me, it was the realization that I didn't know everything."

The voice startled Ava as she spun in her chair, barely keeping it from toppling over.

"Leo! you almost stopped my heart." She chastised him as he let out a small chuckle, a smirk playing along his soft lips.

"I'm sorry, dear. I didn't mean to. The little ones were wondering when Mommy would be by to tuck them in."

Looking back at the window, Ava realized that the sun was almost completely beyond the horizon. "I'm sorry i lost track of time." Standing, she stretched her sore limbs. Her body protested after hours of stagnation.

Leo stepped forward, wrapping his arms around her willowy form. The sun-kissed muscles rippled as he pulled her lightly to him. Letting out a squeak, Ava tumbled against his broad chest. His deep rumbling voice surrounded her. Relaxing her arms, laying them over his and throwing her head back to look into his hazel eyes, she gave him a soft smile.

"How is it going?" Leo's eyes shone with worry and love as he gazed down at her.

"About as bad as I was expecting it to be. I just don't know how to go about this. Too little information and the girl might blow us off. Too much and we could risk a breach." Ava let out a sigh. "I wish Elias were with us."

"He's doing the good work where it's needed." Leo comforted his wife. "How about you go say goodnight to Mica and Emmeline, then we can try to tackle this together?"

Nodding, Ava broke away from Loe and headed out of the study to tuck in her twins. She made her way down the dimly lit hallway, the soft patter of her boots echoing against the rough-hewn walls. As she approached the children's room, the muffled sounds of their laughter and chatter reached her ears, bringing a faint smile to her lips.

"Aren't you supposed to be in bed?" Pushing open the door, Ava was greeted by the sight of her twins, Mica and Emmeline, engaged in a spirited game of make-believe. They looked up at her with bright eyes, their faces alight with the joy of childhood, a stark contrast to the weight that often seemed to burden her own heart. The cheeky smiles they sent her way said they knew they had been caught but didn't care.

"Mommy!" they cried in unison, abandoning their game to rush into her open arms.

Ava enveloped them in a warm embrace. For a fleeting instant, the worries of the rebellion and the burden of her task seemed to fade away, replaced by the pure, uncomplicated love she felt for them. Mica and Emmeline snuggled against her, their small hands clutching the fabric of her jacket. Ava's heart swelled with a fierce protectiveness, a burning desire to shield them from the harsh realities of the world beyond their humble home.

"Hello, my little ones," she murmured, placing gentle kisses on their foreheads. "I'm sorry I'm late. Mommy got a bit caught up with her work, but I'm here now."

"Will you tell us a story, Mommy?" Emmaline asked, her voice barely above a whisper.

Ava hesitated, her mind briefly returning to the letter she had been composing, the weight of its message heavy on her shoulders. But one glance at her children's hopeful faces erased her hesitation, and she nodded.

"Of course, my darlings. What kind of story would you like to hear tonight?"

"The one about the girl in the tunnel." Mica said, his bright hazel eyes reminding her of her husband.

"Alright then. Go get in bed, you two, and then we can start."

Scampering away from her, the two quickly dove into their beds, pulling the covers up to their chins and practically vibrating in their positions with anticipation.

As Ava settled onto the edge of Mica's bed, her hand rested on Emmeline's as she leaned over. She took a deep breath.

"There once was a girl who lived underground, where there was no light or life to be found. Her name was Amelia, and she was trapped within the confines of The UnderPod, a vast network of tunnels and facilities that had become her entire world." The story flowed from Ava's lips as easily as breathing. It was one she had been told as a young woman by Elias. The memories of his storytelling brought a fond smile to her narrow lips. "Despite the sterile and regimented nature of this subterranean existence, Amelia clung to the faint glimmers of hope and creativity that flickered within her."

"What does sterile mean?" Mica asked, popping out from his covers.

Ava paused, smiling at her seven-year-old son and his slight lisp as he tried to say the word. "It's a word used to describe a place so clean it's void of dust." Ava said, trying to remember to use smaller words for her children.

"Ooo" Mica made a face of understanding and settled back into his bed.

"Raised on a steady diet of government-approved education and training, Amelia had always felt a deep longing for something more." Ava continued as she tucked him back in. "She would often escape into the limited selection of books available, her mind wandering to the stories of adventure and self-discovery that lay beyond the boundaries of her underground home." Ava reached over and kissed Emmeline on the forehead, tucking her in as well. "In the quiet moments, she would secretly write in her notebook, capturing the fragments of narratives that blossomed in her imagination, daring to dream of a world where she could freely express herself."

For the next several minutes, Ava's voice filled the room, transporting her children to a world so different from their own—a world where the constraints of their reality were everywhere. Where they couldn't dream, couldn't plan, couldn't think on their own. She watched as their expressions shifted, their imaginations captivated by the story unfolding before them. When the tale came to a close, Mica and Emmeline let out contented sighs, their eyelids growing heavy with sleep. Ava placed one last kiss on each of their foreheads, whispering soft goodnights before quietly slipping out of the room, her mind suddenly clear.

Leo was waiting for her back in the study, his fingers skimming along the words she had written. He was slow, his mouth forming the vowels and syllables as he did so, his reading skill set still growing since his escape from Univo-can seven years ago.

"What do you think?" she was careful to speak up softly, the scars he bore from his time under the hands of The Patrol not all physical.

Leo looked up at her, his eyes focusing back on the present and softening as they always did when he spotted her. It never failed to melt Ava's heart.

"These are good. Lots of information and you reach out with an open hand. What do you feel like you're missing?"

Stepping into the room, Ava made to sit beside him. "I think I've finally figured it out. Will you help dictate to me?"

It was several days later before Ava felt like she finally had a letter worth sending. It wasn't too long—only a couple of pages or so—and the writing was anything but pretty coming from her untrained hand, but it conveyed what needed to be said.

Ava's fingers deftly folded the letter, creasing the paper with precision. She held it in her palm, feeling the weight of the words she had carefully chosen, before slipping it into a weathered envelope. With a steady hand, she wrote the name "666" on the front, a code name that would identify the intended recipient or so she'd been told. Her gaze drifted to the window, where the muted light of the setting sun cast long shadows across the rugged barren terrain that lay past the cities of Univocan. She knew the journey this letter would take would be fraught with danger, but she had to hope it would reach its destination. Turning, she made her way through their home, her footsteps soft and purposeful. She found Leo in the study, hunched over a map, his brow furrowed in concentration.

"The letter is ready," Ava announced, her voice low and serious.

Leo looked up, his hazel eyes reflecting the gravity of the situation. "Are you sure it's the right time to send it?" She knew he was concerned about the recent uptick of patrols along the border of the wastelands and the closest city of Univocan.

Ava nodded, her resolve unwavering. "I've gone over it countless times. And I don't think we can wait any longer. She will be leaving the pod soon and we have no way of knowing where in The Next World she will be assigned. It's the best way to reach her, to plant the seeds now."

Leo reached out, his calloused fingers gently brushing against hers. "I trust your judgment, my love. But the ris k..."

"I know," Ava interrupted, her hand tightening around the envelope. "But there is always a risk with these things."

Leo studied her face for a moment, then sighed. "Very well. I'll make the arrangements. Darius should be able to deliver it to the messenger in time."

Ava felt a surge of relief, but the underlying tension that hung in the air tempered it. She knew that once the letter was sent, there would be no turning back. The rebellion would finally start, and it would have far-reaching consequences, both good and bad.

As Leo made the necessary preparations to leave, Ava found herself drawn to the window once more, her gaze fixed on the distant horizon. In the fading light, she could almost imagine the silhouettes of Univocan and in the skies above the space colonies of The Next World.

"Hold on, 666," she whispered, her words carried away by the gentle breeze. "Help is coming."

Chapter 5

Darius

D arius Kane's boots thudded against the metal grating as he paced the dimly lit confines of the rebel hideout. He furrowed his brow, and his lips formed a terse line. The weight of his thoughts were heavy. It had been ten years since he had found Elias's journal in the home on New Horizon. Ten years since his world had been rocked to its core. He spent several months debating what he was going to do about the journal he had found. Almost handing it over to the authorities more times than he cared to admit. But every time he did, he would hesitate, and read the words again until he found he couldn't justify passing those words on to anyone else. After some debate, he cornered Elias and confronted him.

The man was surprisingly unfazed that someone found out his secret. Giving Darius a look that was to wise for his age, he had simply invited him in for a cup of tea. Two glasses of whiskey later, Darius was looking wide-eyed at Jonal, or Rafe, as he learned was his true name, stepping out of a hidden passage.

"So this is him?" the young man had simply asked. After Elias's confirming nod, Darius's life had changed forever.

His thoughts returned to the present as he entered the grand room of Celestia Station's central hub, looking around. The space was littered with tables. Some were occupied with people eating, others held card games or conversations, and a very select few contained quiet debates about movements and strategies, all in code so the rest of the colony couldn't understand what was really being said. He glanced over to where Elias Marlowe sat, his fingers dancing across a worn notebook as read the notes. The *Writer* now *Reader's* brow was creased in concentration.

"Elias," he called out, drawing the older man's attention to him.

"Darius, how have you been?" Standing, Elias stretched out, his smaller stature twisting and turning with the effort.

Darius approached him with a smile, reaching his hand out to his old friend. "I've been as well as I can be. Gina sends her regards and says you must come by for dinner soon."

Elias let out a deep chuckle, looking up at Darius. "I'll have to take that invite; your wife's cooking is second to none. But I have a feeling you didn't seek me out just to relay that invite."

As always, Elias was more perspective than he let on.

"Yes, I'm here to discuss your recent proposal to the council." Darius watched as Elias's eyes grew hard.

"Follow me." The two weaved out of the main chamber and through the interconnecting halls of the colony base. The soft morning light of the sun coming around the Earth brought with it the chime of the speakers overhead.

"First rounds start at seven a.m." the soft feminine voice unnecessarily reminded the residents around the station.

After about five minutes of walking, the two had made it to one of the more secluded parts of the space station. A corner rarely used by anyone but *Readers*, and even then so few visited its old halls it was practically a ghost town. The old library doors whooshed open with a small creek, and the two stepped inside.

"Alright then, my friend, what is it you would like to discuss?" Elias said once he had ensured the room was clear and had activated a silencing device.

"You can't really believe this girl, this '666,' could be the key to our success?" Darius asked, his deep voice cutting through the silence.

Elias looked up, his mechanical eyes meeting Darius' steady gaze. "I do," he replied, his voice firm. "From what I've been able to piece together, she's a remarkable young woman—one who's been shaped by the very system we're fighting against yet hasn't fully formed to its mold. If we can reach her, if we can show her another way, she could be the catalyst we need to ignite the spark of rebellion."

Darius admired Elias's intellectual prowess, but he also knew that the man's idealism could sometimes cloud his judgment. This was one of those moments he worried age was getting to the man. "She's so young, barely thirteen, and a brand new Podie at that. What could she possibly do for us?"

"She might not be able to help yet, but I believe with the right influences and people in place we could shape her. By the time she is old enough to leave, we could very well have our own axe to cut the system down."

Darius considered Elias's words, his mind racing with the implications. He knew that the rebellion was still in its infancy, a fragile flame the oppressive Univocan regime could easily snuff out. The idea of relying on a single, untested individual made him uneasy, but he also recognized the potential that Elias described.

"And you're certain she's the one?" he asked, crossing his arms over his chest.

Elias nodded, a determined glint in his eye. "I've been monitoring the reports from The UnderPod, and everything I've seen points to her. She's intelligent, curious, and she's already shown a willingness to defy the system. She will be perfect."

"Alright," Darius said slowly, uncrossing his arms and taking a step forward. "I'm willing to try it. But we'll need to be cautious, and we'll need to move quickly. You can not be the one to reach out. Find another who can do the work for you. We can risk losing you and the power you wield here in the open. The Univocan regime is relentless, and it won't hesitate to crush any sign of rebellion. You know that better then most."

Elias nodded, a small sad smile tugging at the corners of his lips. "I understand, Darius. We'll proceed with the utmost care and vigilance. I've already begun making the necessary arrangements. It won't be easy, but I believe it's our best chance of turning the tide."

Darius considered Elias' words, his mind already whirring with the details of their plan. The Univocan regime was not to be underestimated, and it would stop at nothing to maintain its grip on power. "Alright then," he said, his voice low and serious. "Let's get to work."

The two men bent their heads together, their voices hushed as they discussed the specifics of their plan.

Darius stood in the shadows, his eyes narrowed as he scanned the crowded streets of the UnderPod. The air was thick with the hum of machinery and the chatter of the residents, a cacophony that set his nerves on edge. They were treading on dangerous ground, but it was too late now. Elias had convinced him to go see the girl for himself, to see if the first contact had gone as they hoped. Though he disagreed with the old man, he was as stubborn as a mule, and Darius had to give in before he went on his own and put himself in danger. He glanced over at Elias, who stood beside him, his eyes hidden behind the glare of his glasses. The *Writer's* expression was calm and composed, but Darius could sense the tension in his posture.

"Are you sure this is the right place?" he murmured, his voice barely above a whisper.

Elias nodded, his gaze fixed on the bustling crowd. "This is where the reports say she's been spotted the most. She's been given the first letter. If we're going to make contact, this is our best chance."

Darius nodded, his jaw clenching with apprehension. "Alright then," Darius said, his voice low and steady. "Let's do this."

The two men stepped out of the shadows, blending seamlessly into the flow of the crowd. Darius kept his eyes trained on the sea of faces, searching for any sign of the elusive girl they had come to find. As they wove through the throngs of people, he couldn't help but feel a sense of unease. The UnderPod was a tightly controlled environment, and the Univocan regime had eyes and ears everywhere. *This really was the worst plan the old man had thought of in some time*, he thought mirthlessly.

Suddenly, Darius glimpsed a familiar face in the crowd—a young girl with dark, wavy hair and large, expressive eyes. His heart quickened, and he elbowed Elias gently, nodding in the girl's direction.

"That's her," Elias whispered, his own eyes widening with recognition.

Darius nodded, his gaze locked on the girl as she moved through the crowd. She seemed nervous, her eyes darting from side to side, and Darius couldn't help but feel a pang of sympathy for her. He knew all too well the weight of living under the Univocan regime once your eyes had been opened, the constant fear and the need to always be on guard.

Carefully, Darius and Elias followed the girl, keeping a safe distance and blending in with the other residents. As they trailed her, Darius couldn't help but examine her. Despite the oppressive environment, despite the fear she hid, she seemed to carry herself with a quiet determination; her steps sure and her gaze unwavering. He could see the spark of curiosity and defiance in her eyes, and he knew that Elias was right—she could be the key to their success.

Suddenly, the girl turned a corner, disappearing from view. Darius and Elias quickened their pace, rounding the corner just in time to see her slip through a door, the metal frame sliding shut behind her. They exchanged a quick glance, and without a word, Darius stepped forward, his hand reaching for the door. He paused, his fingers hovering over the handle, his mind racing with the implications of what they were about to do.

"Are you sure about this?" he asked, his voice low and serious.

Elias nodded, his expression resolute. "We've come this far, Darius. We can't turn back now."

Darius took a deep breath. They were treading on dangerous ground, but Elias was right; they couldn't afford to let this opportunity slip through their fingers. With a determined nod, he pushed the door open and stepped inside, Elias close on his heels.

The room was dimly lit, the air thick with the scent of old books and the hum of a ancient computer terminal. Darius and Elias stood in the doorway, their eyes adjusting to the low light as they scanned the small, cluttered space. And there, huddled in the corner, was the girl they had been searching for—666, her eyes wide with a mixture of fear and curiosity at the new arrivals in her space.

Elias stepped forward, his hands raised in a gesture of peace. "It's alright," he said, his voice soft and soothing. "We're not here to hurt you. We just want to talk."

The girl's eyes darted between the two men, her body tense and ready to flee.

"My name is Elias," the *Writer* continued, his tone gentle. "And this is Darius. We're... well, we're part of a group that's trying to make things better. We think you might be able to help us."

The girl's brow furrowed, her lips parting as if to speak. But before she could utter a word, the sound of voices echoed from outside, and Darius felt his heart skip a beat. "Someone's coming," he murmured, his eyes narrowing as he scanned the room for a escape route.

"Under my desk."

The two men snapped their heads to the girl as she spoke up for the first time. Her voice was like a razor dripped in honey, sweet yet sharp.

"There's room; it's quite large, but hurry." The girl stepped away from her desk. Darius and Elias quickly hid in the space underneath. If Elias had been any taller, they wouldn't have fit, but luck was on their side for once, and though tight, they made it in time for the knock at the door.

"666?" a male voice called out from the other side of the door. "Are you in there? I thought I heard something."

Darius could just make out the girl from where he hid. Her shoulders tensed as heard the voice, but she forced them to relax, and a tense smile flittered across her pale face.

"809," the tension in her form didn't filter into her voice. "Come in."

The sound of the door opening made Darius and Elias tense.

"Hi." The male's voice was clearer now, a deep, nervous-sounding baritone that traveled across the space. "I didn't mean to intrude. I just wanted to come by and see if you would have dinner together tonight when I thought I heard... another male voice in here."

Darius watched as 666's shoulder slumped, the tension leaving her body as she stepped around the desk.

"That's very sweet of you, 809. I appreciate your looking out for me." There was a lilt to her tone that implied she was trying to flirt with the young man. "As you can see, I'm alone and safe. I would love to attend dinner with you this evening. How does first shift sound?"

The joy in the boy's voice was obvious to Darius even though he couldn't see him. "Really? I mean, yes, first shift sounds perfect. I will meet you at the entrance to escort you."

"I'm looking forward to it."

Darius stayed tense until the door closed with a firm click and the distant sound of footsteps faded from view.

An audible sigh left the girl's mouth moments later as she called out to them. "You can come out; it's safe now. But it's best we keep our voices low."

The two men tumbled from under the desk in an undignified heap, landing at the feet of the girl. She looked down at them, a small smile on the edge of her lips.

"So I'm guessing you're the ones Ava's been talking about?

Chapter 6

Amelia

Amelia's fingers trembled as she gripped the tattered scrap of paper, the words scrawled across it etching themselves into her mind. For weeks, she had pored over the first message, trying to decipher its meaning, its purpose. What did this stranger want from her? Why had the blonde boy chosen her, of all people?

The weight of the paper felt heavier than it should, a burden that she struggled to bear. She had kept it hidden, tucked away in the pages of one of her few books, afraid that its discovery would bring her more trouble than she could handle. But the curiosity that had first sparked within her upon receiving the note had grown into a restless flame, one that demanded to be fed.

Glancing around the cramped living space she shared with her section, Amelia's eyes settled on the small, barred window that offered a glimpse of the system beyond. The system suppressed individuality and heavily regulated the pursuit of knowledge. But if there was one thing Amelia had learned, it was that even in the most tightly constrained environments, there were always cracks through which one could glimpse the possibility of freedom. Her heart raced as she considered her next move. She knew the risks—the consequences of being caught could be severe. But the allure of uncovering the truth, of discovering what lay beyond the confines of her sheltered existence, was too powerful to ignore. With a deep breath, she made her decision.

That evening, as her section gathered for their dinner, Amelia feigned a headache and slipped away, pleading the need for rest. Once inside her empty shared dorm, she quickly changed into darker, more inconspicuous clothing and slipped the folded note into the pocket of her trousers. Carefully, she eased open the window, mindful of the creaking hinges, and began her descent down the narrow alleyway.

The UnderPod was a maze of interconnected passageways and dimly lit corridors, a labyrinth of concrete, dirt, and steel that concealed a multitude of secrets. Amelia moved with practiced ease, her footsteps barely making a sound as she navigated the shadows, her eyes scanning the area for any sign of guards or *Patrols*.

As she drew closer to the holding cells, Amelia's pulse quickened. The air here was thick with tension, the atmosphere charged with an undercurrent of fear and unease. She paused, pressing herself against the cold, damp wall, her senses on high alert. Voices echoed from the distance, and she strained to hear the muffled conversations. Cautiously, Amelia peered around the corner, her heart pounding in her ears. The holding cells were just ahead, their heavy metal doors guarded by a pair of armed sentries. Swallowing hard, she retreated into the shadows, her mind racing to devise a plan.

Time seemed to stretch on as Amelia waited, her eyes scanning the area for any opportunity to slip past the guards unnoticed. Finally, her chance came when a sentry stepped away to take a call on his PortMed. Seizing the moment, Amelia darted forward, her footsteps light and quick, and slipped through the open doorway before the guard returned.

The holding cells were a maze of dimly lit corridors, the air thick with the scent of fear and despair. Amelia's breath caught in her throat as she moved cautiously, her eyes searching for the familiar face of the blond-haired boy who had given her the note. She paused at each cell, peering through the small glass windows, her heart sinking with each empty or unfamiliar face she encountered. Just as

Amelia was about to lose hope, a movement in the corner of her eye caught her attention. Turning, she stared into a pair of piercing blue eyes, the gaze of the blond-haired boy from the note fixed upon her. Amelia felt a surge of relief and trepidation, her fingers instinctively reaching for the crumpled paper in her pocket.

"You came," the boy whispered, his voice barely audible through the thick glass that separated them.

Amelia nodded, her mouth suddenly dry. "I... I wasn't sure what to do. But I had to know what this all meant." She pulled the note from her pocket, her fingers trembling as she held it up for him to see.

The boy's expression shifted, a flicker of hope igniting in his eyes. "Then you understand the importance of what I've asked you to do."

Amelia's brow furrowed, her mind racing. "I don't know what you mean. All this note says is I'm going to free everyone, but it doesn't explain why. What is it you need me to do?"

The boy leaned forward, his face pressing against the glass as he spoke in a hushed, urgent tone. "Get me out of here. I'm part of a resistance movement that's trying to uncover the government's darkest secrets. And you—you're the key to all of this. Your bloodline has been leading this city for generations with its writing before it was outlawed. You were born for this."

Amelia's eyes widened, her heart pounding in her chest. "Me? I'm just... I'm just a girl from The UnderPod. I don't have any power or influence. I don't write." The lie tasted bitter on her tongue.

"We both know that's not true. You don't have to lie to me," the boy said, his voice laced with a sense of urgency. "We have seen your works, the ones you hide in your drawer. No, no, don't look at me like that. No one else knows. Please stay, listen; you're the perfect person to help us—no one would suspect you. You can move freely without drawing attention to yourself. And you have access to information and resources that we desperately need."

Amelia shook her head, her mind reeling. "You've got the wrong girl. I'm not a revolutionary. I can't even miss mandated mealtimes without having a panic attack about it. The other day was a fluke, a... a misstep. It won't happen again... Today is a misstep. New Worlds, what am I even doing here!" Amilia moved to leave, but the boy moved faster, snagging her hand through the bars.

The boy's eyes narrowed, his expression serious. "It's not a misstep, and you know it. Even if you don't admit it out loud, you know in your soul. The government has been suppressing the truth, 666. There is more going on than you know, and none of it is good. If we don't stop the rise of the new regime now, then things are only going to get worse.

Amelia felt a chill run down her spine, the weight of the boy's words sinking in. "But... how? I don't even know where to start. And what if I get caught?"

"You have to trust me," the boy said, his voice urgent. "I know it's a lot to ask, but the fate of our world hangs in the balance. If we don't act now, the government will bury the truth forever."

Amelia's mind raced, her thoughts a whirlwind of fear and uncertainty. She had never imagined herself being thrust into such a dangerous life. But the boy's words had ignited a spark of something within her. Whether she was ready to admit it fully or not, the seeds had been festering for years, even since she was a kid and saw her father lose his *Writer* privilege. Steeling her nerves, Amelia nodded, her gaze meeting the boy's. "Okay. I'll do it. But you have to tell me exactly what I need to do."

The boy's face lit up with a relieved smile, and he quickly began outlining his plan.

An hour later, Amelia was back in her dorm, her mind already racing with a thousand questions and concerns. The journey ahead would be perilous, filled with unknown dangers and obstacles. But for the first time in her life, she felt a sense of purpose that was greater than the mundane life she had before. In her reading room the next day, Amelia carefully hid the note in her book again, her fingers tracing the familiar words. She knew that from this moment on, her life would never be the same. The weight of the mission she had accepted was heavy, but she was determined to see it through.

Three weeks after her talk with the messenger, another letter arrived. Addressed to her by someone named Ava, it held information on all that she would need to start. Amelia sat cross-legged on her narrow bunk, the flickering light of her PortMed casting an ethereal glow on the letter before her. Her fingers traced the more elegant script, the words of this mysterious "Ava" filling her with a sense of purpose and trepidation. As she pored over the detailed instructions, Amelia's heart raced with a mix of excitement and fear. Over the next few months, she dedicated herself to the task at hand, meticulously studying the layout of The UnderPod and memorizing the schedules of the *Killers* and *Patrols*. She spent countless hours in the government-sanctioned library, scouring the limited texts for any clues or insights that could aid her mission.

As she delved deeper into her research, Amelia uncovered troubling patterns—discrepancies in the official narratives, unexplained disappearances, and whispers of dissent that the government had long sought to suppress. Ava's letters helped harden her resolve, fueled by a growing determination to expose the truth and give voice to those who had been silenced.

Amelia's days became a delicate dance as she worked to maintain an outward mask of compliance. One day, as she sat in her reading room, working late and avoiding others as she liked, she heard a soft knock at her door. Holding her breath, she crept to the entrance and peered through the peephole, her heart leaping when she recognized #809.

"666?" #809's voice was barely above a whisper. "Are you awake? I need to talk to you."

Amelia hesitated for a moment, her fingers tightening around the doorknob. She knew the risks of letting anyone into her room, especially someone as inquisitive and observant as #809. But the earnest plea in his voice compelled her to unlock the door and usher her inside.

"What's wrong?" She asked, her brow furrowed with concern.

#809 glanced around the small room, his eyes lingering on the PortMed that still flickered. "I... I've noticed you've been acting strange lately. You're sneaking off, and you seem distracted during our sessions."

Amelia's heart raced as she tried to formulate a response, but #809 continued before she could speak.

"I'm worried about you. I know things haven't been easy for you, not since that frightful day in Sector 99, but I can't shake the feeling that you're involved in something dangerous." #809 reached out and grasped Amelia's hand, his eyes shining with something Amelia had worked hard not to acknowledge. She felt a lump form in her throat, refusing to meet his gaze. She had always valued #809's friendship, and the thought of betraying that trust weighed heavily on her.

"I... I'm sorry, #809," she said, her voice trembling slightly. "I can't tell you what's going on. It's... it's complicated."

#809's brow furrowed, and he squeezed Amelia's hand tighter. "666? Please let me help you."

Amelia shook her head, her gaze dropping to the floor. "Really, it's nothing. Trust me, okay?"

#809 opened her mouth to protest, but Amelia quickly raised a hand to silence him. "Please, #809. Just... just promise me. I..." she paused, knowing she would probably come to regret the words coming from her mouth as she swallowed down the guilt. "I have been working to ask you out."

#809 dropped Amelia's hand, stepping back to study her face. "Do you really mean that?" His voice was hopeful, but his expression portrayed the skepticism he felt.

Amelia knew there were far worse fates than dating and possibly falling in love with a man like #809. He was everything a girl could want, patient, smart, kind. The flash of a blonde-headed boy in her mind was quickly pushed aside. He was nothing but a fleeting fantasy, a desire in her heart for a life more adventurous than the one she had once had.

"Yes, I mean it."

The smile on #809's face could have lightened any room.

Chapter 7

Elias

E lias star at the official letter in his hand, sealed with the symbol of Univocan with a mixture of surprise and trepidation. Ripping the paper open he read the words on the page. They seemed to blur as his mind raced, trying to comprehend the implications of this sudden promotion.

Just a few weeks ago, Elias had been a *Writer*, his days filled with the quiet contemplation of the written word and the crafting of stories that explored the complexities of Univocan society. But now, in the wake of the *Reconstruction*, his profession had been deemed obsolete, and he had been reassigned to the role of *Reader*. something that grated at the twenty-two-year-old. The transition had been difficult, to say the least. Elias had been forced to abandon his beloved craft, the one that had brought him such fulfillment and purpose, for one of complacency. He had watched helplessly as his fellow *Writers* were stripped of their livelihoods, their works censored and destroyed, their dreams crushed in the government's relentless campaign to erase the past.

Now, as he stared at the letter, Elias couldn't help but feel a glimmer of hope. The promotion to a higher position within the *Readers'* ranks promised greater access to information, a chance to delve deeper into the inner workings of the Univocan government. Perhaps with this newfound vantage point, he could uncover valuable intelligence that could aid the growing rebellion.

Following the instructions in his letter, he headed to the Building of The Keepers. The interior of the building was a study in stark, utilitarian design—no trace of the warmth and creativity that had once defined Univocan's public spaces. Following the directions, Elias navigated the maze of corridors until he reached a nondescript door, where his future awaited. With a deep breath, he stepped inside, his eyes adjusting to the dimly lit room. At the far end, a lone figure sat behind a large desk, its features obscured by the shadows.

"Elias Marlowe," a deep, authoritative voice spoke, "we've been expecting you."

Elias straightened his posture, his heart pounding in his chest. "I'm here as requested, sir."

The figure leaned forward, revealing a severe-looking man with a sharp, angular face and piercing eyes. "You've been selected for a new role, one that will require your unique skills and abilities."

Elias felt a glimmer of hope, but he tempered his excitement, unsure of what to expect. "I'm honored to serve Univocan in any way I can."

The man nodded, his expression unreadable. "The Reconstruction has brought many changes to our society, and we find ourselves in need of individuals who can navigate the complexities of this new era." He paused, his gaze scrutinizing Elias. "You were a Writer, were you not?"

"Yes, sir," Elias replied, his voice steady despite the unease he felt at the admission.

"And you were considered one of the most talented among your peers," the man continued, a hint of approval in his tone. "Your way with words, your understanding of the human condition—these are qualities we believe will serve us well in the role we have in mind for you."

Elias felt a tightness in his chest. The *Writers* had been vilified during the *Reconstruction*, their work deemed a threat to the stability of Univocan. To be singled out and praised for his abilities was unexpected, and he couldn't help but wonder what the true motivation behind this offer might be.

"I'm...I'm grateful for the opportunity," Elias said, choosing his words carefully. "What exactly is this new role you have in mind?"

The man leaned back in his chair, steepling his fingers. "You are to become a Keeper of Readers."

Elias blinked, his mind racing to process the implications of this new assignment. It was a position of power and influence, one that Elias had never imagined himself occupying.

"A Keeper?" he echoed, unable to conceal his surprise.

"Yes," the man affirmed, a faint smile tugging at the corners of his lips. "Your skills as a Writer will be invaluable in this role. You will be responsible for which of the government's messages make it to the Readers, ensuring that our vision for Univocan is clearly understood and embraced."

Elias felt a knot forming in the pit of his stomach. The idea of being a mouthpiece for the very system that had dismantled the *Writers'* profession, the one he was working to rip down, was deeply unsettling. And yet, he couldn't ignore the potential this position held.

"I understand," he said, his voice measured. "What will be expected of me in this new role?"

"You will have access to a wealth of information and resources few others know," the man explained, leaning forward once more. "It is expected that this information will stay as it is, a secret. You will also be expected to act in the best interest of Univocan, no matter the cost."

Elias nodded, his mind racing with the implications of this new possibility. "And what of the remaining Writers? So many are still looking for work. What will become of those who did not convert to Readers or Speakers?"

The man's expression darkened. "That is not your concern, but if you must know... the Writers who have refused to realize the errors of their ways will be... delt with."

Elias felt a chill run down his spine. The tone in the man's voice was a stark reminder of the consequences of defying the new order. The thought of being complicit in the suppression of his former colleagues was deeply unsettling. He needed to figure out what he could do for them before it was too late and without breaking his cover.

"I see," he said, his voice barely above a whisper. "And what if I were to... have reservations about this role?"

The man's eyes narrowed, a hint of warning in his gaze. "I would advise against such thoughts, Elias. The Reconstruction has brought about necessary changes, and we expect all citizens to embrace their assigned roles for the good of Univocan."

Elias swallowed hard. "Of course, sir. I will do my utmost to serve the government and the people to the best of my ability." He stood tall, hoping to portray the stature of a man honored and humbled by the offer.

"Excellent," the man said, a satisfied smile spreading across his face. "Your first assignment will be to deliver a speech at the upcoming public gathering, outlining the government's vision for the future of Univocan."

Elias felt a sense of dread wash over him, but he nodded in acquiescence. "I understand. When do I start?"

"Immediately," the man replied, standing from his desk. "Your training will commence tomorrow morning. Congratulations, Elias Marlowe. You have been chosen to play a vital role in shaping the future of our society."

Elias forced a smile, his mind racing with a whirlwind of emotions. "I'm honored sir." As he left the dimly lit office, he couldn't help but wonder if he had just made a deal with the devil to try and kill him.

The next few weeks were a blur of intensive training and preparation. Elias found himself immersed in a world of data, statistics, and carefully crafted talking points, all designed to mold him into the perfect government mouthpiece. Throughout it all, his unease grew. He had been a *Writer*, a chronicler of Univocan's rich cultural heritage, a creator of worlds one could only imagine. Now he was a tool of propaganda, a conduit for the government's agenda. His days were filled with lectures on the intricacies of Univocan's new policies, the importance of military might, and the necessity of absolute loyalty to the state. He was drilled in the art of public speaking, learning to project confidence and authority, even when the words he spoke felt like a betrayal of his own beliefs. Even though he was slowly helping to undermine the society, who knew how long until the rebellion could take root, could truly move? How long would he have to pretend?

The day of his first event arrived, and Elias found himself on the stage, facing a sea of expectant faces. People knew him, trusted him, and he was about to lie to their faces. He took a deep breath, his eyes scanning the crowd, and spoke. His words flowed with practiced ease, conveying the government's vision for a stronger, more unified Univocan. He extolled the virtues of military might, the importance of obedience and loyalty, and the need for every citizen to embrace their assigned roles. As he spoke, Elias could feel the weight of his words, the way they pressed down on his conscience. He had worded his speech carefully. To the untrained ear, it was everything that his new bosses wanted. But to those whom the resistance had reached, who met in the dark of night, whispering plans for the freedom of all, it was a call to action.

When the speech concluded, the audience erupted in thunderous applause, and Elias felt a surge of pride. No

Killers were heading his way. No *Patrol* calling for his head. He had done it; he had successfully navigated the treacherous waters of his new role. As he stepped down from the stage, he glimpsed a familiar face in the crowd. It was Mara, a fellow *Writer* who had been his closest friend and confidante. Elias saw a flicker of disappointment and betrayal in her gaze. The look felt like a stab to the heart. He had hoped to reach out to her sooner rather than later and bring her into the fold, but he now knew he would have to send another to do it. She would no longer trust the words coming from his mouth, at least not for now.

In the days that followed, Elias found himself immersed in a whirlwind of activity. He was assigned to a team of *Readers*, tasked with interpreting and disseminating a steady stream of government directives and reports. He delved deeper into his work, each day another step into the void. He noticed the subtle shift in the information he was receiving. Certain details he was told were being omitted, key figures were being erased from the historical record, and the government's messaging was becoming increasingly focused on military might and national security.

One day, as he pored over a stack of classified documents, a particular report caught his eye. It detailed the fate of the *Writers*, those who had not conformed. The language was vague, but the implications were chilling.

Elias froze. The window for his group to move had shrunk. They needed to act, and act fast. Quickly he got to his feet, determined to let Darius, his most recent recruit, know.

What if it's *a trap?* The thought halted his movements. It was a possibility he couldn't ignore. This could be a test of his loyalty. So few knew this information, and of them he was the only *Writer*, the only one with ties to these people and a desire to save them. No, as much as he hated to admit it, he would have to be careful. To bide his time and ensure the information was not only accurate but that any connections to him when the time came to act were hidden.

Over the following days, Elias gathered information, piecing together a mosaic of truth that lay beneath the surface of the Reconstruction. He reached out to old contacts, former *Writers* who had been scattered to the far corners of Univocan, and together they uncovered the darker truths that the government sought to conceal. Piece by piece he confirmed that, yes, it had been a trap, but all the same there was a plan to eliminate those who opposed the new status quo and he could prevent it with the right moves.

One evening, as Elias was poring over his notes, a knock came at his door. His heart raced as he cautiously approached, unsure of who might be on the other side. To his surprise, it was Mara, her eyes shining with a mixture of fear and resolve.

"Elias," she whispered, her voice barely audible. "I know what you've been doing. I want to help."

Elias felt a surge of relief and trepidation. He knew others had contacted her, and he had heard that they were successful in their recruitment, but he never dreamed she would come to him. He felt a wave of conflicting emotions. On one hand, he was grateful to have an ally, someone he could trust to help him in his quest for the truth. But on the other, he couldn't help but worry about the consequences they would both face if they were discovered.

"Mara, you have no idea the kind of danger you're putting yourself in," he said, his voice laced with concern. "The government, they're...they're not to be trifled with. If they find out what we're doing, the consequences could be severe."

Mara's eyes narrowed, a steely determination etched into her features. "I know the risks, Elias. But I can't just sit back and watch as they erase our history, our culture. We have to do something."

"Alright," he said reluctantly. "But we have to be careful. I don't want to risk your life unnecessarily. I care to much about you."

Mara blushed at his admission, a glimmer of hope and determination in her eyes. "I'm with you, Elias. Whatever it takes, we'll uncover the truth and expose the government's lies."

Chapter 8

Ava

*B*ANG.

Ava's heart pounded as she spun toward the front door. Acting on instinct, she shoved her children behind her. The handle on the door turned, and before she could act, it swung open. The sight of Leo bruised and bloody ripped a scream from her throat. Stumbling forward, she barely caught him before he collapsed.

"Close the door quickly," she commanded her children, and the two scurried to do as she said. Ava dragged Leo into the bathroom. She made quick work of stripping off his shirt and cleaning his wounds to assess the damage.

"Mommy, is Daddy okay?" Mica asked.

"I don't know, dear." Ava looked over her passed-out husband, trying to hide her fear from her children. Thankfully, the more she cleaned him, the more apparent it became that his injuries were minimal, and the blood was most likely not his. Shooing her children away, she changed and dressed Leo, too small and tired to drag him elsewhere. She carefully laid him on the bathroom floor and waited.

What felt like hours later, he finally stirred, drawing Ava's head up from between her legs and skittering toward him.

"Where am I?" His voice was hoarse, a groan accompanying his question.

"You're safe, you're home," Ava practically cried the words, tears falling onto his chest as she pulled a sitting Leo into a hug.

He relaxed into her embrace, his shoulder shaking softly, his hands gripped her shirt tightly.

Dear 666,

I hope my previous letter reached you safely and brought a glimmer of hope amid the darkness that surrounds you. In this second letter, I want to tell you more about the world beyond Univocan—and the people who are fighting for your freedom.

Out here, beyond the confines of The UnderPod and the towering cities, we are a diverse gathering of individuals.

Each of us carries our own story, our own scars, and our own reasons for rebelling against the government's control. We come from every walk of life, united by one shared belief: that every person deserves the right to choose their own path.

*One of the most inspiring figures in our resistance is a man named **Elias Marlowe**. He was once a renowned Writer—a master of the written word who used his craft to awaken and challenge the minds of Univocan's people. When the government moved to eradicate the Writers and their influence, Elias was faced with a choice. Instead of bowing to their will, he rose above it.*

Elias is an old man now. The lines on his face tell the story of struggle and sacrifice, yet his spirit remains unbroken. His resolve burns as fiercely as ever. He is the one who entrusted me with these letters, believing that your voice, 666, could become the spark that ignites the change we have long awaited.

Elias understands the true power of words—their ability to inspire, to challenge, and to transform. He has devoted his life to mastering that power, studying how language can ignite the human spirit. Now, he passes that knowledge to you, hoping you will use it to kindle the flames of rebellion within the UnderPod.

I know it may seem impossible, but I believe in you, 666. I believe the same spark that drives our rebellion burns within you too. With Elias's wisdom and the strength of our grow-

ing movement behind you, I know you can help tear down the walls of conformity and lead our people toward freedom.

In the letters to come, I will share more of our strategies, our plans, and the stories of those who have already risked everything for the cause. But for now, hold tight to this truth: we are fighting for you. And the day of our liberation is closer than you might think.

Stay strong, 666. Keep your mind open. Trust in the written word—it may yet be the key to our salvation.

Yours in the struggle for freedom,
Ava

Ava carefully folded the second letter and placed it on her desk, sealing it with the wax stamp. The reports about the girl relieved her. She had yet to contact her but hoped that 666 was curious enough for them to reach out again.

With a deep breath, she stood from her desk and crossed the hall to the small living space; her gaze drifted to her twins on the couch. Mica and Emmeline slept peacefully, clueless to the troubles of the world beyond their walls. She wanted them to stay that way. To grow up in a world free from the shackles of government control, where they could pursue their own dreams and aspirations without fear of retribution.

Ava gently brushed a stray lock of hair from Emmeline's forehead, her heart swelling with a mixture of love and determination. "For you, my darlings," she whispered, "and for all the children of Univocan, we will succeed."

Turning away from the sleeping children, Ava made her way to the door, slipping the letter into the pocket of her jacket. She needed to deliver the letter to the messenger before sunrise. The cool night air felt pleasant against her brow. The movement drew her eyes to Leo, who was leaning on the wall of their home, staring into the night.

Leo still curled slightly to his left, the bandages under his shirt distorting it, his injuries still healing. He was lost in thought before his wife's movements caught his eye. He turned his attention to Ava, his dark eyes full of concern. Pushing off, he reached out to give her a gentle hug.

"Are you sure about this, Ava?" he asked, his voice low and steady.

Ava nodded, her gaze resolute. "I am. It's best you don't meet the new messenger since your face has been associated with the last one."

Leo sighed, his grip tightening momentarily before he released her hand. "Then I trust your judgment. Just be careful, my love. The Patrol is always watching, and I can't afford to lose you."

Ava offered him a small, reassuring smile. "I'll be careful. And I'll make sure the letter reaches its destination safely."

Dear 666,

These last few letters had been small windows into our world. Today I'm sliding you a map.

You know what lies beyond the UnderPod now, to lie out how we get you out of it. Elias and the others have stitched together a plan—dangerous, precise, and built on the smallest of chances. It will demand courage, secrecy, and steady hands. I believe with everything I have that it's the way out.

At the heart of the plan is a simple truth: words can open locked places. Elias spent years tracing Univocan's seams—its schedules, its blind spots, the places its machines and minds forget to watch. From those seams, he found possibilities. From those possibilities, he found you.

The government tried to bury the Writers, to hollow out their influence and leave only echoing obedience. In that hollow, they created a vacancy—an empty space begging to be filled. Your voice, 666, could be the shape that fills it. Elias imagines your words as more than whispers: a tide that pulls at the foundations of their control and drags us back toward a world where people choose their own paths.

No more UnderPod. No more forced implants, no more transfers to The Next World. Choices. Books, speech, living *on your own terms—those small luxuries we once took for granted. That is what we aim to restore.*

This is not a request so much as a summons. If you accept, you must trust the power inside you and be willing to risk everything to use it. I won't lie—the risk is real. The window of opportunity is narrow. We've enclosed Elias's drafts and the outline of our approach; read them. Memorize. Burn them. Above all, be ready.

We move quietly. We move together. The future is not given—we write it, line by line. Make sure the first line you write is worth the rest.

Yours in the dark and the dawn,
Ava

Ava carefully placed the fourth letter into the hands of her new messenger. With a determined nod, the young man tucked it into his jacket and turned to leave. She watched him go with a mix of fear and admiration.

Dear 666,

As I write this letter, I feel the weight of the trust we've placed in you. The plan we've outlined is demanding, and the responsibility it carries is heavy—but I believe in your strength and courage. Your last letter reached me during a difficult time, and knowing you are finding your voice has meant everything. Now I must share the final piece of the puzzle, the part that will decide whether our mission succeeds.

Darius has spent countless hours studying the UnderPod's schematics, dissecting its security and hunting for weaknesses. He's convinced the heart of the system—the central data hub where all information and communication are routed and monitored—is the key to our infiltration.

This is where you will have the greatest impact. If you can gain access to that hub, you can disrupt the government's control, seed doubt, and broadcast our messages of hope and defiance straight to the people who need them. To do it, you'll need to earn the trust of the managers and The Director. Prove yourself a Keeper of Readers.

I won't pretend the risks are small. They are real and serious. But so is my confidence in you.

In the coming days, trusted members of our network will reach out with the tools and instructions you'll need. Follow their guidance—and trust your instincts.

The time to act is now. We stand for the right to choose our own paths and to write our own stories. Go forward with steady hands and clear purpose.

May the written word guide you, and may the spirit of our cause burn bright in your heart.

Yours in the struggle for freedom,
Ava

Ava watched the letter disappear on the horizon with the man who carried it. It would be the last before 666 would leave The UnderPod and head to The New World in six months' time.

Weeks later, she sat at her desk, fingers drumming against the worn wooden surface. A soft sigh escaped her lips as she leaned back in her chair, her gaze drifting to the window. She knew it was going to take sometime for the next steps to go into action, but she felt like she should have heard something already. The sound of footsteps in the hallway drew her attention, and she straightened in her chair, her body tensing in anticipation. Leo knocked before he entered, his face unreadable.

"Any news?" She asked, her voice low, as if she were afraid that speaking any louder would bring bad news.

Leo's face softened, with a small smile. "They've made contact. 666 has been getting your letters and making preparations. Elias and Darius are there now. Their cover for being in The UnderPod to recruit the most promising of the Readers has gone without a hitch, and they plan to launch the first strike in a few days."

The tension in Ava's shoulders released, and she collapsed into her chair. "Thank goodness." She sighed.

Leo stepped around her, placing a gentle hand on her shoulder. "You did well." He kissed the top of her head. "A year's work all coming to its conclusion. How do you feel?"

Ava stopped to think for a moment. "Stressed, content, lost. I don't know. After this, it's all out of our hands, you know. Neither of us are fighters or a politicians, all we can do is sit back and watch."

Chapter 9

Coming Together

Ava's boots crunched against the rocky terrain as she made her way towards the hidden rebel outpost. The weight of the holo-pad in her jacket pocket served as a constant reminder of the message it contained—a rallying cry for the people of Univocan to rise against the oppressive regime.

Gripping the strap of her pack, Ava scanned the horizon, her sharp eyes searching for any signs of movement or potential threats. As she approached the outpost, she spotted Elias and Darius standing guard at the entrance, their postures tense but alert. Ava raised her hand in greeting, and the two men quickly recognized her, their expressions shifting to one of relief.

"Ava, you made it," Elias said, his voice low but warm. "We've been waiting for you."

Darius nodded, his gaze sweeping the area behind Ava. "Any trouble on the way?"

"Nothing I couldn't handle," Ava replied, a hint of a smile tugging at the corner of her mouth. She glanced at the holo-pad in her pocket, the weight of its contents heavy on her mind. "Is everything ready?"

Elias and Darius exchanged a brief look before Elias spoke up. "Yes, the transmission is scheduled to go out in a few hours. We've made the preparations, but there's still one crucial step we need your help with. We know you aren't a fighter, and we don't want to put you in danger, but the member we were going to rely on got stopped at the border."

Ava's brow furrowed slightly.

Darius stepped forward, a light in his eyes. "We need someone to record the transmission. To hold the line when the Killers eventually show."

Ava felt a surge of trepidation. "Leo would be better for this job. He at least understands angles and such as a former Speaker."

"We know," Elias stepped for his wrinkled hand resting on her shoulder. "But Leo is helping prepare for the after. Please, we wouldn't ask if we weren't desperate."

Ava hesitated and then nodded. "Okay, I'll do it."

"Oh, good, because I was hoping after almost two years I wasn't about to be let down by my mentor," a soft feminine voice called out.

Ava's attention turned to the figure stepping out from the side of the building. The girl was a few years older than the images she had last seen of her, yet she knew her all the same.

"Amelia," the name came out with excited relief. After all their years of communication, she had finally met the one she could call her best friend in person.

"Hey Ava," Amelia said with a shy smile, tucking her shoulder-length hair behind her ear. "What's up?"

Ava's arms were around her before she could finish speaking, squeezing the life out of the young woman. "God, it feels amazing to finally see you in person." She stepped back reluctantly as she smiled. "But let's catch up later, okay? We've got a lot of work to do."

"We don't have much time." Darius said. "The Hackers will rig the broadcast soon. We need to have the recording ready for them by then."

"Alright then, let's do this." Ava nodded.

Elias stepped forward, placing two worn hands on Amelia's shoulders. "Are you ready, my dear?"

The girl shook slightly under the weight of his touch. A touch she had been denied all her life. One she only heard about through tales from her father. Even after three years of visits, it still felt like a forbidden gift. "Yes, grandfather." Amelia's voice cracked slightly at the word, but her eyes were misty with love.

The four of them made their way into the abandoned outpost, the dim lighting casting shadows across the makeshift control room. The equipment was ancient but still functional. Elias quickly set up the recording equipment, his nimble fingers working with practiced efficiency.

"Okay, Amelia, we're ready when you are," he said, gesturing to the small camera.

Amelia steeled herself, stepping in front of the camera, her gaze focused and unwavering.

"This is Amelia, speaking on behalf of the Resistance. I come to you today not as a Reader, not as a recent Podie Grad, but as a girl, a daughter, a granddaughter, a fellow citizen," she began, her voice clear. "I beg you to listen to me. For too long, we have lived under the oppressive rule of the Univocan government, our freedoms stripped away, our voices silenced. How many friends have you watched disappear after the evaluations? How many families have been ripped apart and sent scattered across The New World? Does this not sound like history repeating itself? Our teachers warn us of the fallout of The Great School Wars from the 2120s. They tell us of the dangers of oppression, of division, yet they have done the same thing to us, using the need to populate the stars as a excuse for our separation." Amelia paused to take a shuttering breath her eyes blazing at the camera.

"Today, I stand before you with a message of hope and a call to action." She spoke of the atrocities committed by the regime, the harsh realities of life outside the regulated zones, and the burning desire for true liberty. Her message was a rallying cry, a defiant challenge to the powers that had for so long held the people of Univocan in their grip.

Elias and Darius listened intently, their expressions a mix of pride and determination. Years of hard work had finally paid off.

Elias couldn't help but feel a surge of pride seeing his granddaughter, a child he had only heard of from distant letters his son sent as the government tossed him across the solar system, refusing to let him return home to family. standing up for their future. Three years ago he had taken a chance, had pressed the resistance to trust his blood despite having never met her at that point. Three years ago, he had held her in his arms for the first time after sneaking into her reading room in The UnderPod. Now he was watching her, a young woman two years out of the space, leading the future of their people.

Ava stood beside the men, a burden seeming to lift from her shoulders with every word Amelia spoke.

When Amelia finished, a heavy silence fell over the room.

Then Darius let out a shuttering breath and nodded, running a hand through graying hair. "That's the take. By The New World, it definitely hits different in person, with your voice," he said.

Elias quickly reviewed the footage, nodding in approval. "All the players are in place. We need to get this to the Broadcast Tower in the next thirty minutes," he said, his voice tinged with a sense of both hope and trepidation.

The four of them sprang into action. The holo-disk was shoved into Darius's pocket, Ava ran to prepare the transport's coordinates, and Amelia helped Elias to the pad. He flickered out of existence moments later, appearing in the empty broadcast tower moments later. Stepping out of the way, the others joined him. Thousands of credits, favors, and blackmail had been used to empty the space for the precious few moments they needed in order to get their Transmission out. Much of it was made easier by Ava gaining the title Keeper of Readers, like her grandfather before her.

Darius moved to the panel before them, slamming it open as a drawer of holo-disks popped out. He inserted their recording and shoved it back in, typing on his PortMed to the Hackers they were ready. "The transmission is set to go out," he said to the other three, his eyes flashing to the door on the far side of the tower's main room and then around the abandoned equipment. HEW stepped back hand falling to his service weapon as he waited.

"It's all come to this," Amelia said. "To think only three years ago the two of you were tumbling from under my desk in The UnderPod."

Darius and Elias exchanged smirks at the memory.

"Are you ready?" Elias asked Ava, the wrinkles around his eyes even more prominent as he smiled.

With a resolute nod, she replied, "I'm ready."

As the countdown began, Ava couldn't help but feel a sense of foreboding. After Univocan ceased to exist as they knew it, what would happen? She knew, of course, the plans they had laid out to ensure a peaceful transition into a new government. But she also knew that things rarely ever went according to plan.

Amelia sighed beside her, as if sensing her thoughts, reaching out to grab the older woman's hand in comfort. The equipment hummed as it broadcast the signal across the Univocan network. Everyone's eyes were fixed on the monitors as they waited for the first signs of the message reaching its intended audience.

Suddenly, the screens erupted with a flurry of activity, notifications and alerts flooding the system. Ava's heart raced as she watched the message being shared and discussed across the Univocan network. The hacked feeds coming from holo-pads, PortMeds, even bus stops, showed the faces of the citizens to the solar system. The people's reactions ranged from shock and disbelief to a growing sense of hope and determination as others seemed to straighten.

"It's working," Darius murmured, a glimmer of pride in his voice. "They see it. I knew it. Elias, you were right; people have been starving for this. For freedom."

Elias let out a breath he didn't realize he was holding, a small smile tugging at the corners of his mouth. "Ava, Amelia, your message has struck a chord. The people are listening."

Ava was exhilarated. They had done it; they had ignited a spark of rebellion that she hoped would soon become a raging fire. But as the initial excitement subsided, her concerns took root.

"What happens now?" Amelia asked, her gaze shifting between Elias and Darius, mirroring Ava's worries.

"The transmission is out. The government will retaliate, but our people should take up the charge. The cells are ready to move at the slightest sign of acceptance. Our people are spread across every planet, moon, base in the system," Darius said finally, sagging into a chair, his age showing for once.

Just as Elias was about to respond, a boom filled the air. Seconds later, the building shook from the impact of what could only have been a U-Bolter.

"They found us already?" The fear in Amelia's voice shot through Ava as she turned to Darius. He was out of his chair, typing away furiously on the console. The screen before them changed, the front cameras coming up to display the streets outside the broadcast tower. In the distance, they saw a small platoon of *Killers* approaching, with a tank in the middle.

"BotJuice," Darius swore.

"What are we going to do?" Amelia asked.

Darius turned to Elias, and Ava watched as they silently communicated. With a determined nod, Darius turned to the two women.

"*We* aren't going to do anything," he said firmly. "You two are going to get out of here while we distract them so you can get away."

"Ho—"

"No arguments, my dear," Elias said, stopping Amelia with a gentle hand on her shoulder.

She grabbed the weathered thing as if it were her only lifeline. "I can't leave you. I just got you back," she pleaded with him.

Ava had to look away, feeling as though she was intruding on a private moment.

"I know, my dear, but we all knew the risks when we chose this path in life. Besides, I've lived to a nice old age. You, on the other hand, are still young with a lot to offer the world. I lost your father too young. I don't wish to bury another child."

"But, Grandpa—"

"Please look after her, Ava."

Ava whipped her head around to make eye contact with Elias. Those wise old eyes, which for years had held a burning flame, now had a soft ember.

"I will." Ava nodded, her eyes shining with unshed tears as she grabbed onto Amelia's hand. With a final, silent exchange, she turned and made her way towards the exit, dragging a protesting Amelia along, her heart heavy but her resolve unwavering.

As Ava disappeared into the darkness, Elias and Darius exchanged a weighted look.

"One last fight, old friend?" Elias asked.

"I'm right here with you." Darius moved to the console, his fingers flying across the screens as he worked to secure their position and prepare for the impending onslaught. Elias took a deep breath, his gaze fixed on the door through which Ava and Amelia had vanished.

"May God be with her," he murmured, a silent prayer for the young woman who had become the symbol of their rebellion. For the last of his line. Suddenly, the alarms blared, warning of a breach.

"Get ready, Elias." Darius growled, his hands gripping the handle of his weapon.

Elias nodded, his own weapon at the ready. "For the rebellion," he said, his voice low and resolute.

As the first wave of Univocan soldiers breached the outpost, Elias and Darius took aim.

The sound of Bolter fire echoed through the corridors, the clash of metal as weapons met improvised shields and the cries of the wounded filling the air. Elias and Darius fought with a ferocity born of desperation, their every move calculated and precise as they sought to buy the women as much time as possible. But the Univocan forces were relentless, their numbers and resources overwhelming. Slowly but surely, they lost ground, their ammunition running low and their bodies growing weary.

Elias glimpsed a familiar face among the Univocan soldiers—a former rebellion comrade, now turned traitor. The realization hit him like a physical blow; that was why they had been found so fast.

"Darius," he gasped, his voice strained. "It's Rafe. He's leading the assault."

Darius's eyes widened, a flash of anger and disbelief crossing his features. "That Glitching Mother—," he growled, cutting himself off, his grip tightening on his weapon.

Elias, his breathing heavy, turned to Darius, his expression grave. "We need to buy the girls more time. We can't hold them off much longer."

Darius nodded, his jaw set with grim determination. "Then let's make sure they remember this day," he said, his voice low and resolute.

The two gave one final push, Darius leading the charge with a cry, his Bolter unloading into the men before him. Before they could make it too far, a shot rang out louder than the rest. Like watching in slow motion, Darius saw Elias fall. The barrel of the Bolter pointed at him in Rafe's hands. With a roar of rage and grief, Darius charged towards him, his weapon blazing.

Caught off guard by his fury, Rafe stumbled back, his own weapon failing just long enough for Darius to punch into his defenses and tackle him to the ground. The two men engaged in a fierce, close-quarters battle, their movements a blur of steel and determination. It didn't last long. Darius felt the Bolts entering his body as Rafe dislodged him and fired. He tumbled to the ground.

"You chose the wrong side, Rafe," he wheezed out as the younger man stumbled forward.

"We'll see about that," Rafe spat out, aiming his gun at Darius's head. "Any last words?

"Long live The Unbound."

Chapter 10

The End and The Beginning

T he sun had barely peeked over the horizon, casting a warm glow across the bustling city of Univocan. In a modest apartment near the heart of the city, Ava and Leo stirred from their sleep. Ava turned to face her husband. Her hair a wild tangle of dark curls and graying lines as she stretched her arms overhead, her scars from the war faintly visible in the soft light. Leo pulled her in as she admitted a soft squeak. Squeezing her tight and placing a kiss on her forehead.

"Another day," Ava murmured, her voice laced with a hint of wistfulness.

"Another chance," Leo replied, his hazel eyes reflecting the same determination that had carried them through the rebellion, the war.

The two got ready, heading to make breakfast for their family. It would be the last day the unit would live together under one roof. The twins were off to vocational school. The sound of footsteps echoed down the hall, and soon the twins, Mica and Emmeline, emerged from their rooms, their faces alight with anticipation. At nearly eighteen years old, they were on the cusp of adulthood. Their gangly limbs and awkward forms of their teenage years had slowly given way to shapely, strong forms.

"Morning, you two," Leo greeted them with a warm smile. "Sleep well?"

Mica, the elder twin by a mere five minutes, nodded enthusiastically. "Couldn't wait to start the day," he said, his voice brimming with excitement.

Emmeline clasped her hands together, her eyes shining with a mixture of nerves and excitement. "Do you think we're ready, Mom? Dad?" she asked, her voice laced with uncertainty.

Ava moved to her daughter's side, wrapping a comforting arm around her shoulders. "You've been preparing for this for years," she reassured her. "Whatever you choose, you've got this."

Leo joined them, placing a hand on Mica's shoulder. "Your mother's right. You two have the skills and the passion to find your place in this new Univocan. We're so proud of you. Whatever dream you pursue, you can know it's one you alone chose."

Mica nodded, his expression filled with resolve. "I'm ready to take it on. I want to make a difference, to help create a better future for Univocan."

Emmeline's lips curled into a tentative smile. "And I can't wait to share my stories, to inspire people and help them see the world in a new light."

The twins exchanged a glance, their expressions reflecting the uncertainty of what lay ahead even as their bodies vibrated with anticipation. Mica reached out and squeezed Emmeline's hand, offering her a reassuring smile.

"Let's do this," he said, his voice filled with determination.

The family left their apartment together, stepping out into the bustling city below. The central square of Univocan was alive with energy, a bustling hub of activity as the Vocational Placement Ceremony unfolded. From all corners the crowd surged, other young adults spilling into the square eager to head off to the vocational schools in The Next Worlds. As Ava and Leo watched their children disappear into the crowd of the other graduating students, they couldn't help but feel a bittersweet pang in their hearts. The journey that had brought them to this moment had been arduous, filled with countless sacrifices and hard-won victories. Thousands of lives had been lost in the war—close friends, families, allies. But now, as they saw their children poised to embark on their own paths, they knew that the future they had fought for was finally within reach.

Ava and Leo made their way through the throngs of people until they found their seats beside some of their oldest friends. Amelia greeted them with a smile, her new husband exchanging a kind but wary glance their way. The man once known as #806 now called Henry had always felt that The Unbound asked too much of his wife to young but he had never been openly hostile to the cause and supported her even when he learned her heart for many years had belonged to another. The blonde boy who had sparked it all for Amelia had died saving Henry's life on Europa, and two years of fighting and healing later, had found him and Amelia truly in love. Between the two now sat their oldest daughter, Marcy, named after Henry's mother; their middle son, James, named after Amelia's father; and their youngest, Elias.

As the ceremony started, Ava squeezed Leo's hand, her heart swelling with pride and anticipation. "There they are," she whispered, her gaze fixed on their children.

Leo nodded, his own expression mirroring Ava's. "They look so grown up," he murmured, his voice tinged with a hint of wistfulness.

The twins stood tall, their faces a mix of nervousness determination as they awaited their turn to be called forward. One by one, their peers stepped up to the podium, their choices announced to the cheering crowd. Some chose paths in the sciences, others in the arts or skilled trades—a testament to the newfound freedom that had blossomed in Univocan.

Finally, Mica's name was called, and he strode confidently to the front, his head held high. Ava and Leo leaned forward, their breath caught in their throats, as the official read out Mica's chosen vocation.

"Mica Mercer has chosen to pursue a career in engineering, specializing in sustainable energy solutions," the official announced, eliciting a round of enthusiastic applause from the crowd.

Ava couldn't help but grin, her eyes shining with pride. "That's our boy," she murmured, squeezing Leo's hand tightly.

Leo beamed, his own heart swelling with joy. "I knew he had it in him," he said, his voice filled with conviction.

As Mica stepped back into the crowd, Emmeline's name was called, and she stepped forward, her hands trembling slightly.

"Emmeline Mercer has chosen to pursue a career in the arts, with a focus on creative writing and storytelling," the official announced, eliciting a wave of cheers and applause.

Emmeline's face lit up with a radiant smile, and Ava felt her own eyes fill with tears of joy. "That's my girl," she whispered, her voice thick with emotion.

Leo wrapped his arm around Ava, pulling her close, his own eyes glistening with unshed tears.

Ava nodded, her gaze fixed on her children as they rejoined the crowd, their faces alight with a sense of accomplishment and excitement. "They're going to change the world, Leo," she murmured, her voice filled with conviction.

As the ceremony drew to a close, Ava and Leo made their way through the throngs of people, embracing their children.

"We're so proud of you both," Ava said, her voice thick with emotion. "You've worked so hard, and you deserve this."

Leo nodded in agreement, his gaze filled with affection. "Your choices reflect your passions and your dedication. We know you're going to do amazing things."

Mica and Emmeline exchanged a glance.

"It's just... it's all happening so fast," Emmeline admitted, her brow furrowed with uncertainty. "What if we're not ready?"

Ava placed a reassuring hand on her daughter's shoulder. "You are ready, and every time you feel you aren't, we are right here, just a teleporter hop away. Now it's time for you to go. Celebrate with your peers. We'll see you tomorrow before you head off to New Horizon."

Leo chimed in, his voice warm and encouraging. "Remember, we're here for you every step of the way. This is just the beginning of a new chapter, and we'll be right by your side. No one will ever be able to take that from us."

The twins took one shaky breath, then hugged their parents and darted off.

The two watched them go before Ava and Leo turned and walked hand in hand through the bustling streets of the Univocan city. Their footsteps carried them to familiar haunts and hidden corners of the city they now called home. The once rigidly controlled metropolis had undergone a transformation in the last five years since the war, its once-sterile façade now adorned with vibrant murals, street vendors, and the lively chatter of its liberated inhabitants.

As the sun set, Leo stopped to watch, his hand tightening in Ava's. "Can you believe it's been eight years since the broadcast?" He mused, his gaze sweeping over the ever-changing landscape.

Ava nodded, his expression pensive. "It feels like a lifetime ago, and yet only minutes. The battles, the constant fear of being discovered, the sacrifices..." She paused, her eyes darkening with the weight of those recollections.

Leo gave her hand a gentle squeeze, offering him a reassuring smile. "But look at what we've accomplished. Univocan is changing. The people are free to choose their own paths, to pursue their passions. It's not perfect, but it's a far cry from the rigid, oppressive system we fought against. Elias would be proud."

Ava's lips curled into a small, proud smile. "You're right. I just wish he had been here to see it."

As the evening drew to a close, they stepped into the quiet living room of their home. The emptiness that lingered with the lack of children was almost too much to bear, but Ava knew they would make it through the changes ahead and persevere just like they always had.

Meanwhile, five years after the rebellion won, Amelia and Henry walked their own path home, their children skipping and tumbling in front of them. Amelia had always been drawn to the power of words, her secret notebooks filled with fragments of stories and musings that yearned to be set free. During the tumultuous years after the broadcast, during the war, she had struggled with balance, the impact and power her words could bring. It was in her darkest moments, after losing her first love, when she felt like she was drowning, that she had discovered the three most powerful words of all.

I am here.

Henry had been a sturdy rock in her life. Despite the lies she had originally told him, how she had loved another, and the uncertainty she had felt about him, he had never wavered. He was a quiet but passionate man who shared her love for the written word and held a love for her hotter than the sun.

I love you were the sweetest words Amelia had ever known, and she would cherish every day she got to say them to him and hear them back. Now, their three children, six-year-old Marcy, four-year-old James, and one-year-old Elias—were proof of that love.

As they neared their home, Amelia slowed her steps, watching her children chase one another down the quiet street, their laughter echoing through the evening air. Henry's hand found hers, warm and steady, grounding her in the present. For so long, her words had been weapons—tools of rebellion, of loss, of survival. But now, they had become something gentler: a means of healing, of hope, of love. She looked at her family, free and alive, and felt a peace she had never thought possible. The rebellion had given them freedom, but love had given that freedom meaning. Henry caught her gaze and smiled, the kind that said everything words couldn't. Amelia exhaled, soft and snorted.

"We are not having another," she said to the unspoken promise in his eyes, but even as she said the words she knew she didn't mean them. "Fine, maybe one more, but not for at least another year," she acquiesced with a soft smile and roll of her eyes, following her husband and family in.

The world was still imperfect, still scarred, but for the first time in her life, she no longer felt the need to fight it. Instead, she would write it—one story, one moment, one heartbeat at a time.